PENGUIN WORKSHOP
An imprint of Penguin Random House LLC
1745 Broadway, New York, New York 10019

First published in the United States of America by Penguin Workshop,
an imprint of Penguin Random House LLC, 2025

Text and the illustrations on pages ii, iii, 280, and 281
copyright © 2025 by Rob Renzetti
All other illustrations copyright © 2025 by Penguin Random House LLC

Illustrations by M. S. Corley, except illustrations
on pages ii, iii, 280, and 281 by Rob Renzetti

Photo credit: Paper texture: Miodrag Kitanovic/iStock/Getty Images

Penguin Random House values and supports copyright. Copyright fuels creativity, encourages diverse voices, promotes free speech, and creates a vibrant culture. Thank you for buying an authorized edition of this book and for complying with copyright laws by not reproducing, scanning, or distributing any part of it in any form without permission. You are supporting writers and allowing Penguin Random House to continue to publish books for every reader. Please note that no part of this book may be used or reproduced in any manner for the purpose of training artificial intelligence technologies or systems.

PENGUIN is a registered trademark and PENGUIN WORKSHOP is a trademark of Penguin Books Ltd, and the W colophon is a registered trademark of Penguin Random House LLC.

Visit us online at penguinrandomhouse.com.

Library of Congress Cataloging-in-Publication Data is available.

Printed in the United States of America

ISBN 9780593519592 (paperback)
ISBN 9780593519585 (library binding)

1st Printing

LSCC

Design by Mary Claire Cruz

This book is a work of fiction. Any references to historical events, real people, or real places are used fictitiously. Other names, characters, places, and events are products of the author's imagination, and any resemblance to actual events or places or persons, living or dead, is entirely coincidental.

The authorized representative in the EU for product safety and compliance is Penguin Random House Ireland, Morrison Chambers, 32 Nassau Street, Dublin D02 YH68, Ireland, https://eu-contact.penguin.ie.

**TO MY BROTHERS, BRAD AND TOM.
I WISH WE'D HAD MORE TIME
TOGETHER ON THIS JOURNEY.**

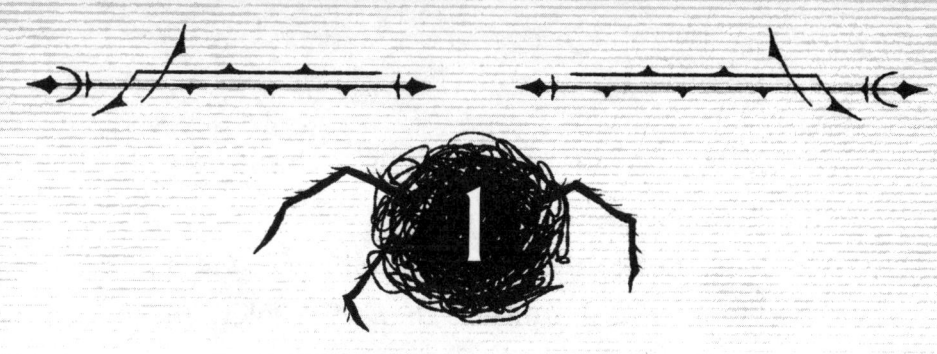

Pursuit

THE BAG SCREAMED. When he looked down at the bag in his arms, he could have sworn that it screamed. He dropped it and ran faster up the slope on the edge of Whichway Woods.

His pursuers gained on him. Long-legged Raggedy Albert and well-conditioned Musclehead led the pack. But Loose Lips, Stickyfingers, and the rest of the rebels were close behind.

Zenith Maelstrom trained his eyes on the hill ahead, lest he slip on the dark green moss. But something darker appeared—the shadow of a gigantic raven. Zenith looked up as Hugh dove at him and grazed his head with the tip of one powerful wing. As the bird soared away, giggles escaped from the small child perched upon his wide neck.

His sister, Apogee, laughing at the plight of her big brother.

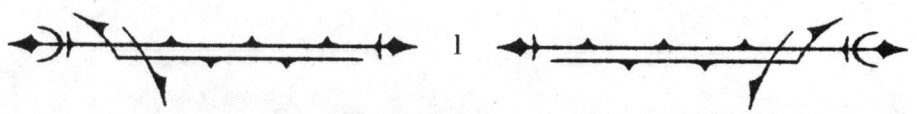

Zenith reached the top of the hill and saw the three foul mouths cackling at him. In front of these portals sat the horrible bag. Impossible. He'd dropped it halfway down the hill. A change of color, an obscene blush, rippled across its haphazardly stitched surface. The bag's mouth opened wide into a grin, and a terrible thing arose from within. A blood-red cloak, covered in cryptic symbols. The phantom's cowl was drawn tightly around one of Four Eyes's eyeballs, now a milky gray, corrupted by the spectral presence floating before him.

The awful, unfathomable Wraith.

Observation

"**INTERESTING**," **DR. VENNELLER** said as he slid his eyeglasses back up his nose and jotted in his notebook. "In prior dreams, this 'horrible bag' is the gateway to the world of monsters. But now the bag itself has made an appearance in—" He flipped back to the previous page. "GrahBhag."

Zenith slumped in his chair, cracks in the leather irritating his neck. "Yeah, well, it *is* a dream."

The psychologist looked up. "I wouldn't be so dismissive. Understanding these dreams could be the key to unlocking your memory and finding your sister." Zenith nodded his head but allowed his mind to wander as Venneller launched into his usual lecture about repressed memories.

There was no reason to listen. Zenith's memories weren't repressed. He recalled every painful moment of his two adventures in GrahBhag, although he'd

fabricated the chase he'd related today. He'd improvised the story to get through the "recount your latest dream" portion of his twice-weekly therapy session as quickly as possible.

What a change from a month ago, when Venneller had discovered the journal, containing the actual details of Zenith's time in GrahBhag, protruding from his backpack. Zenith was horrified when the therapist insisted he read it aloud, but Venneller assumed Zenith was recounting a dream. Zenith found it surprisingly therapeutic to share some of the ordeal he'd survived without fear of repercussions. In the following sessions, he enthusiastically relayed his whole history with the horrible bag, from its mysterious appearance on his front porch through every twist and turn of the two adventures inside.

He didn't tell his psychologist that his last trip had ended when he'd exited the bag in a police evidence locker. After a few panicked minutes trying to escape from the locked cage, he'd been discovered by a sergeant who'd asked how he'd gotten in there.

Zenith had opened his mouth, hoping his brain would come up with something. A simple "I don't know" was all it could manage.

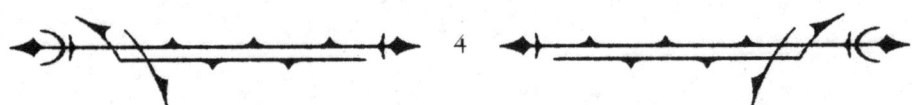

It was enough. On a hunch, the sergeant brought him to the detective interviewing his parents, who had contacted the police after finding the horrible bag, but not their children, at home. After many tearful hugs and kisses, the questions commenced. Where had Zenith been? What had happened? Where were Apogee and Kevin? All Zenith could think to say was, "I don't know."

His parents' frustration at this response evaporated when his mother spotted the A-shaped scar on his wrist. His father asked who had done this to him. Zenith thought, *A cloaked specter called the Wraith burned it into my wrist*, but again said, "I don't know." The questions ceased and hugs resumed.

The police and Zenith's parents reached their own conclusions. Someone had taken Zenith, Apogee, and their friend Kevin Churl. (Sort of true.) Zenith had escaped. (Actually, he'd been ejected.) The traumatic experience had wiped Zenith's memory. (Just the opposite—he remembered everything.)

The sessions with Dr. Venneller were meant to help Zenith remember events that, in reality, he'd never forgotten. Zenith had uttered "I don't know" and "I don't remember" many times in that first

session before Venneller discovered what they now called his "dream journal." Initially, it was easy to fill the hour with talk of GrahBhag, but the thrill of sharing his experiences had since dwindled. The therapy sessions were pure theater meant to satisfy his parents and the police, while his true work was done each night before bed, writing the account of his two trips to GrahBhag and sketching the horrible bag on each page. These pictures seemed to hold the key to retaining his memory. He kept his journal open on his nightstand so he would see an image of the bag first thing in the morning, and, just to be safe, he'd taped Apogee's drawings of GrahBhag up on the walls of his bedroom. He knew from experience that if he were ever to wake without seeing the horrible bag in some form, he'd forget everything. Then Apogee and Kevin might be gone forever.

There was an awkward silence as Venneller waited for a response. Zenith straightened in his chair. "I'm sorry, could you repeat that?"

The therapist scooted his glasses back up his nose. "It's difficult to bring into focus, isn't it? I think we should explore other ways to uncover what your

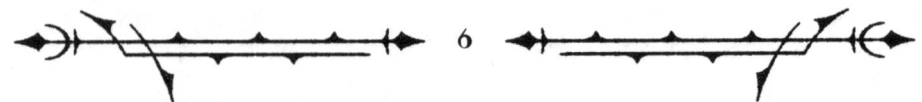

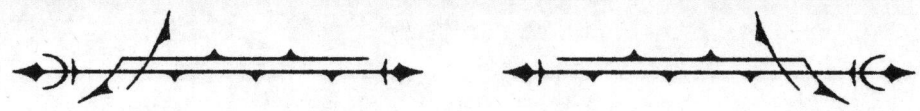

mind so badly wants to conceal. I'm going to speak to your parents again about hypnosis."

Zenith squirmed in his seat. "Hypnosis? I thought we decided against—"

"We'll revisit all this next week." Venneller rose from his seat and ushered Zenith out.

Fish Out of Water

ZENITH WAITED FOR his mom on the bench outside Dr. Venneller's building. Through the large lobby window, he could see the receptionist, who gave him a wan smile. He would've preferred to walk home, but his parents wouldn't allow it. Their searches of the town and the woods beyond had yielded no clues to his sister's or Kevin's whereabouts. The whole community was on high alert. The police assumed the abduction of Zenith, Apogee, and Kevin was connected to a spate of child disappearances in the tri-state area that had started when a girl from Zenith's school, Carol Briar, had vanished more than a year ago. Since Zenith had returned, he'd been strictly supervised, in case whoever had snatched him tried again.

His parents treated him gently, but their questions were unending, as was their grief. His dad spent

hours staring out the living room window. His mom wandered the house half the night, then dozed on the couch all afternoon, clutching a pair of Apogee's pajamas, the cheery star-and-rainbow pattern a stark contrast to the gloom pervading the home. Zenith wished he could alleviate their suffering, but the unbelievable truth would only compound it. So he maintained his charade. This small gap between the end of his therapy session and his mom's arrival was his only chance to be alone with his thoughts and drop the traumatized amnesiac act.

How would his act stand up under hypnosis? If Venneller probed Zenith's psyche and discovered Zenith believed in the literal existence of GrahBhag and all the madness it contained, then what? An invitation to spend the rest of summer vacation in a padded cell?

If that happened, Zenith would never find Apogee and Kevin. Not that he had any idea how to reach them as things currently stood. The horrible bag was locked away in the police evidence locker. Even if he was lucky enough to gain access to it and climb inside, the foul mouths were still sealed shut with Stickyfingers's blue goo-glue.

He was certain it had been Apogee's idea to lock him out of GrahBhag. But why had she insisted on staying in that treacherous world with the vengeful Wraith and countless other horrors? To use her favorite dig at him, she was "too smart to be so stupid." Why was she so desperate to age herself up again? And why and how had she ever journeyed to GrahBhag and used the Collectory's chalkboard magic to change herself into a teenager in the first place? Was it really so she could be the bossy older sister? Zenith knew there must be more to it than that. She'd said she *needed* to be the older sibling. But what could Zenith have possibly done to make that necessary? Perhaps she would've told him if he hadn't insisted they come home without first hearing her out. His stubbornness had been returned in kind by his determined sister, who'd used her newfound allies to overpower and exile him.

And now, while weeks had passed on Earth, years had gone by on GrahBhag. He had no idea what had become of Apogee or his friend Kevin, who'd been badly wounded the last time Zenith had seen him. If only Zenith could turn back time and do things differently. Or somehow reunite with

Apogee and Kevin, assuming they were still alive.

Why had he wanted to be alone with his thoughts? His thoughts were jerks, pointing out how hopeless everything was. He felt like screaming in frustration.

Someone beat him to it. A gruff but nonetheless feminine voice cried out as a low musical tone sounded from behind him. A torrent of water gushed from the alley, overflowing the curb and settling in a large pothole ten feet from Zenith. He could see something writhing in the shallow pool.

It appeared to be a piece of lava rock flopping around. Walking over to the pothole, Zenith could discern the creature's craggy fins and tail. Its three eyeballs bulged. The rocklike fish raised its leathery lips above the water's surface and gasped, "Help me."

Salty Mouth

ZENITH GLANCED INSIDE his therapist's building and saw the receptionist was occupied with a phone call. He scooped up the fish and some water in his cupped hands. His new passenger pointed toward the alley with one stony fin and croaked, "In there—quickly!"

Zenith entered the narrow alley, then stopped. Halfway down was a large black dumpster. Beyond it, the alley terminated in a tall brick wall. In the middle of that wall, several feet above the ground, was a horizontal crevice that couldn't be accounted for by any defect in the bricklayer's workmanship. It was a ragged rip in the fabric of reality. It was a foul mouth.

The mouth coughed up more water, which surged through the alley, soaking Zenith's sneakers. She spat

to clear her throat, then shouted, "You! Flesh-thing! Where the ampersand am I?"

Zenith was too stunned to answer, or move, until the fish in his hands said, "Hurry! Take me to her." Zenith inched his way down the alley. "I said hurry!"

Instead, Zenith stopped abruptly as the mouth in the wall disgorged another batch of briny-looking water. The living portal said, "Where have I ended up, you asterisk?"

Zenith asked, "Are you trying to curse at me?"

"What's my salty language got to do with it? I'm asking which world I'm marooned on."

The fish splashed some of its precious water onto Zenith's face. "Please, Firman! Send me back." It pointed toward the interdimensional rift in the wall. Zenith tossed the fish into Salty Mouth, who took no notice.

"Firman? Did I hear that right? Am I on octothorping Terra Firmament?"

"Uh, yeah." Zenith bent to retrieve a tiny octopus with four tentacles. A quadropus? He lobbed it back into Salty Mouth.

"Of all the lightning bolts and hammers," cursed

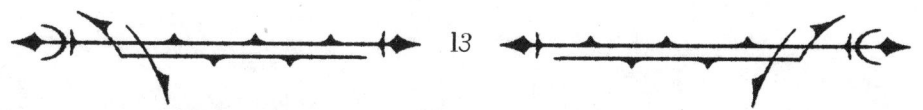

Salty. "Planet's three-fourths water, and I end up on dry land."

"How *did* you end up here?" Zenith edged closer but kept to the side to avoid getting doused. "Did someone smear blood on the wall, or—"

"What the crossbones are you talking about? Wait, I gotcha. You're confusing me with my bloodthirsty cousins. The ones that link your home with GrahBhag. I got nothing to do with that disreputable lot. Spent my whole life at sea. At the *bottom* of the sea in a sunken treasure chest on the aquatic planet of Grawlix. I'm *supposed* to connect that world with the Scalding Sea on GrahBhag."

Zenith was flummoxed. "There's another world besides GrahBhag?"

"There are *many* worlds, you ignorant asterisk. And the links between them have gone haywire. My connection to GrahBhag hasn't wavered yet, but on this end? I've been hijacked to a half dozen different swirly-lined worlds. None to my liking." As if to demonstrate her disgust, Salty Mouth made several heaving noises, but didn't dispel any more water.

Instead, an orange tentacle, over a foot in diameter, undulated forth. Salty Mouth retched and

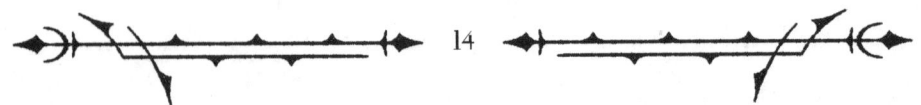

stretched as the enormous tentacle wiggled its way into the world, coiling onto the asphalt of the alley, seemingly infinite in length. But Zenith was certain the tentacle was finite, and that the sea beast attached to the other end would be gigantic.

Multunus

THE TENTACLE WAS indeed finite, but there was no sea beast attached to the other end. There was nothing connected to it at all. It was just a tremendous, disembodied tentacle.

Salty Mouth said, "Oh, for percentage's sake, now we've got to deal with a multunus?"

"Where's the rest of it?" asked Zenith.

"What do you mean, 'the rest of it'?"

One end of the tentacle rose up, revealing an underside with numerous pink suckers. In the middle of each was a mouth. Some mouths displayed square teeth, while others flashed sharp fangs. All screeched at once in discordant, earsplitting voices.

"Hvor dónde wou kie where zkhuh dove ham nasaan koko er estamos si ni are duh kahaan ba wa vi nosotras mir estas we zh siamo he tayo doko?"

"Shut it!" said Salty Mouth. The opposite end of

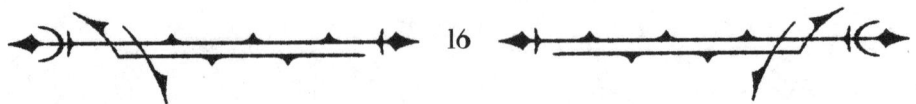

the tentacle rose up and revealed suckers with ears, some fleshy and others fur-lined. "You've spilled into Terra Firmament. In an Anglish-speaking land. So cut the cacophony and use one language."

The multunus's sucker-mouths scoured the ground for water. But then a few near the upraised tip spoke in unison. "So little essence. We must have more!"

"More water?" said Salty. "Ask the Firman."

The tentacle's two ends lowered to the ground, pushing its middle skyward, like a titanic inchworm. Several dozen sucker-noses, some blunt and others pointy, sniffed the air. The sea beast seemed to smell Zenith. It recoiled, but then leaned forward. "The Firman's land-stink is strong, but underneath"— *sniff*—"yes. It has the essence inside."

The creature's mouth-end reared up, baring all its teeth, square and sharp alike. It lunged at the boy blindly, since without eyes, it had no other way to lunge. Zenith barely dodged the sudden attack. The multunus hit the ground mouths-first, and several of the beast's teeth skittered away as Zenith ran toward the alley's opening. The tentacle's ears swiveled, tracking the direction of his footsteps. Then it

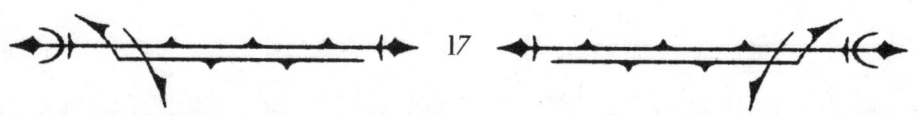

spiraled in upon itself and rolled after him.

Zenith would be clear of the alley before the creature could catch him. He had a good chance of losing the multunus in the well-known streets of his hometown. But that would leave some unsuspecting stranger open to attack.

Stifling a frustrated groan, Zenith ran back into the alley, around the spinning sea beast, which uncoiled, breathing heavily. "Stay still! We must partake of your essence." The flesh surrounding several of its sucker-mouths had turned blue.

Zenith stopped near Salty Mouth, talking low. "How long can this thing last in the open air?"

The foul mouth doused Zenith with seawater. "What now? Speak up, you silly asterisk."

Zenith darted out of the way as the multunus rolled toward the loud mouth. Frantic, the tentacle-beast slurped up the new puddles of water, creating enough noise for Zenith to climb into the dumpster without being detected. Closing the lid, he was assaulted by a fog of fetid cheese and soiled kitty litter. Holding his salty, sea-soaked shirt over his nose provided some relief as Zenith crouched among the garbage.

The multunus cried out, "Firman? Where have you gone? We need your essence, lest we perish."

Perish. Please perish, thought Zenith.

Guttural growling began from inside the bin, and two glowing eyes glared at him. Zenith imagined various GrahBhagian creatures, but what arose on its haunches was an ordinary raccoon. An angry raccoon baring its ordinary, sharp teeth.

Something slammed into the dumpster, knocking it over and spilling Zenith, the raccoon, and the rubbish onto the asphalt. The multunus lunged, two sucker-mouths biting into the shrieking raccoon and pulling the poor creature in opposing directions. Zenith rolled away, not wanting to witness the deadly tug-of-war, and burrowed into the trash heap.

Unsated, the multunus sifted through the pile, frantically chomping on everything in its quest to find life-sustaining liquid. By the time it located Zenith, its complexion had turned a deep blue, and most of its mouths were clogged with garbage. But one free mouth bit his arm, its blunt incisors bruising but not breaking the skin. Zenith yanked his arm free and shoved a crumpled milk carton into the mouth. Another sucker-mouth spat out a beer can, belched, and bared gleaming fangs. Zenith crammed a Styrofoam cup into the open maw.

Zenith continued this debris defense until the thrashing of the GrahBhagian sea beast slowed, then ceased. Exhausted, Zenith collapsed and thought, *I will never, ever play Whac-A-Mole again.*

Plunge

ZENITH HAD TWO or three things to bury. Two if counting species, three if counting distinct parts. He used his foot to push some trash on top of the raccoon's two halves, then took one look at the enormous multunus and decided to let waste management deal with it, despite the shock and confusion it would cause.

As Salty Mouth disgorged more seawater, Zenith stepped forward into the spray, rinsing the dumpster grime from his clothes. He asked, "So the other side of you, it's definitely connected to GrahBhag?"

"Is my Anglish not plain enough?" said Salty Mouth. "My backside remains at the bottom of the Scalding Sea, at least for now."

Zenith grew worried. "You think that might change?"

"It might," said Salty Mouth. "It's all but certain

I'll soon vanish from here and pop up on some other octothorping planet."

Zenith scratched the scar above his left ear. This might be his only chance to return to GrahBhag and find Apogee and Kevin. Of course, it wouldn't help anyone if he drowned or was eaten at the bottom of the Scalding Sea. But after the incident on the pond in Kalikov Park, he'd taken swim lessons. He was a stronger swimmer now and could hold his breath for a long time. If he could avoid any hostile beasts, he was confident he could make it to the surface.

Zenith heard an approaching vehicle and saw his mother's maroon hatchback zip past the alley. Her brakes squealed, then his mother called out, anxious, "Zenith? Where are you?"

He had an absurd desire to come clean. *Here in the alley, Mom. Just vanquished a ravenous tentacle-beast. Now I'm going to vanish through a talking portal to another world. If I'm lucky, Apogee, Kevin, and I will be home for dinner. See you soon!*

Instead, Zenith backed up, inhaled deeply, sprinted toward the brick wall, and dove into the foul mouth.

Hot Water

ZENITH EXPECTED THE gravitational U-turn he'd experienced when traveling through Dry Mouth. But passing through Salty Mouth felt like riding a wave, then being dragged by an undertow. He rocketed through the blackness, only to be pulled halfway back from whence he came. Then forward and backward again. The third surge spat him out of the portal and into the depths of the Scalding Sea.

The sea vent from which he emerged was the size and shape of Salty Mouth. Branching out from each end of the portal, a raggedly stitched seam ran along the ocean floor, with coral on one side and sand on the other. Scanning for signs of danger, Zenith swam slowly upward, his clothes weighing him down.

He shed his jacket, kicked off his shoes, and resumed swimming. He made steady progress toward the surface, but as his body rose, so did the water's temperature: first warm, then hot, then searing. It felt like his exposed skin was melting away. His nostrils were ablaze. His eyes bulged and felt ready to burst. There was no way he would make it to the surface without being cooked alive. Zenith dove back down. He had no choice but to retreat through the portal back to Earth.

As he approached the sea vent, the stitched seam on either side of it vibrated violently. The tremor radiated outward along the seabed, destabilizing the coral, agitating the sand, and clouding the water with debris. A harsh, high-pitched tone sliced into Zenith's eardrums. He clamped his hands over his ears and pressed his lips together to stop himself from screaming and expelling his breath.

The ringing mercifully ended, and the water cleared. But the sea vent was gone. The gap in the seam was now stitched shut.

Zenith knew he couldn't hold his breath much longer. Should he drown at the bottom of the ocean or boil on top? He had taken the name of the Scalding Sea to be metaphoric rather than literal, and it looked like that mistake would cost him his life.

Fish Lips

ZENITH GAZED TOWARD the faraway lime green surface, then back at the emerald water surrounding him. As the very last molecules of air deserted his aching lungs, a gray veil clouded his vision, ruining the pleasing color scheme of his demise.

Through the haze, a shadow approached. He fancied it was a mermaid. But, this being GrahBhag, the creature was more likely to be his doom than his salvation. He imagined it sinking needle-shaped teeth into his throat.

Instead, a pair of leathery lips latched on to his mouth and fed him a fresh lungful of air. The gray veil lifted to reveal the three bulging eyes of the black stony-skinned fish he'd saved in the alley. Their liplock lasted a moment more, then his savior swam away, gesturing with one craggy fin for Zenith to follow.

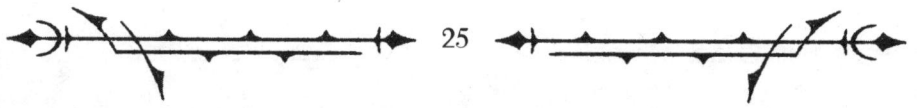

The fish seemed to know Zenith couldn't swim to the surface. Instead, it led him to a long trench, motioning for him to swim within the protection of its walls. The fish darted back up to the surface, then swiftly returned with another infusion of oxygen. In this way, the two swam across the bottom of the ocean.

Zenith had encountered many bloodcurdling GrahBhagian creatures, but he'd never seen such a dizzying array of diabolical beasts as the ones at the bottom of this sea. There were stingrays with six stingers, colossal crabs brandishing claws as sharp as sabers, and wide-mouthed sharks displaying teeth larger and sharper than those of their fiercest earthly cousins.

Ahead of them, in the middle of an outcropping of red seaweed, was another sea vent with a steady stream of bubbles shooting straight up from the ocean floor. Zenith kicked harder toward what he hoped was another portal back home.

Icy water from the vent stung his face. He instinctively shut his eyes and was quickly ensnared by a fishing net concealed amid the seaweed. The mesh closed tightly around him and the fish, its stony

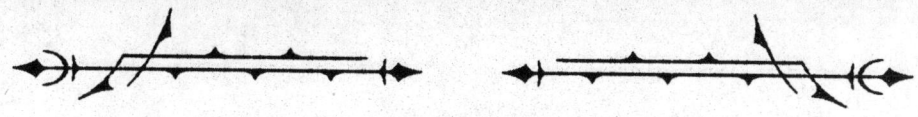

skin digging into Zenith's thigh as the net pulled them toward the surface. A particular panic seized Zenith, one he'd felt once before, when he'd plunged through the ice into the freezing waters of Kalikov Pond. Except this time, death waited above, rather than below. Zenith thrashed wildly, trying to break free before being boiled alive. His struggle was short-lived, as the gray veil descended again and his limbs went limp.

Catch of the Day

*T*HE AFTERLIFE IS *smelly*, thought Zenith. He opened his eyes. *And dark.* A hood, densely woven, covered his head, and a gag filled his mouth. His wrists and ankles were bound, and he lay on his back, sandwiched between what felt, and stank, like two large fish. He'd blacked out in the net but had apparently made it to the surface without suffocating or burning to death. Of course, being bound and gagged was not a promising development.

He heard the buzz of voices around him. Two of them were near enough to be distinguishable.

"I'm telling you, Hurzah, it's cheap at twice the price. See for yourself." The voice was melodious, like a snake charmer's flute.

"What am I looking at, Semblov?" A deeper voice, skeptical.

"That's queen crab," said Semblov. "From the

depths of the Scalding Sea. It's hauled to the surface through a powerful plume of icy water. Keeps those deep-sea delicacies from boiling and spoiling."

Hurzah scoffed. "Hardly worth the effort. It's all claw and no meat."

"The claw *contains* the meat. Never mind. My more discerning customers will appreciate this rarity."

"They're welcome to it." Hurzah's voice came closer. "Is that gourdfish?"

Semblov tittered nervously. "Don't go back there, please. It's off-limits."

"And who do we have here?" The hood was yanked from Zenith's head.

Before Zenith stood a green-skinned creature. Two reptilian eyes dominated the upper half of its broad face. In place of a nose there were three vertical slits. A forked tongue slid across its bloated lips. "You've been hiding the catch of the day."

"Come now, Hurzah." A tarp was thrown over Zenith. "You know our kind doesn't eat Firman. That creature is of no value and not for sale."

That's a relief, thought Zenith.

Hurzah laughed. "Not for sale? You're selling

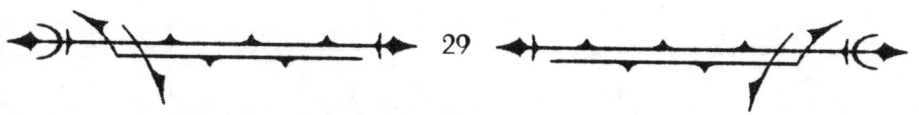

him, all right, and for a hefty price. That's the Dread Outlaw Maelstrom, number two on the Royal Guard's most wanted list. The scar on his wrist is quite distinctive."

That's . . . not a relief.

"Quiet," hissed Semblov. "What is it you want, Hurzah, son of Zurhah?"

"Sem, why so formal? Are we not old friends? And shouldn't friends share in each other's good fortune?"

"And how much of my good fortune am I expected to share, old friend?"

"We'll divide things equally. Let's see, there's you and me. Plus my lifemate and our two podlings. So, five shares, divided equally."

"You pond scum. I'll divide you equally!"

Zenith heard a shriek, followed by the clashing of blades. His table was bumped, then toppled. He tumbled along with the rest of the catch, rolling free of the tarp.

He came to rest facing Hurzah and another creature of its kind, presumably Semblov. Both lay with eyes closed, bleeding, a dagger and scimitar nearby. Zenith scooted along the ground, grabbed

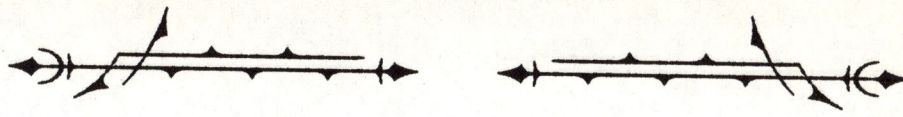

the curved knife, and pressed the blade against the ropes binding his wrists. The scimitar made quick work of the restraints. Zenith stood up and studied the unmoving creatures, wondering whether they were beyond help.

Someone called out, "Sem, you all right? We heard a scuffle." Various beings crowded into the narrow alley housing Semblov's stall. The throng stopped abruptly when they caught sight of the grisly scene and Zenith, still clutching the knife.

"Could that be . . . the Dread Outlaw Maelstrom?" said the tallest one.

"He's killed Hurzah and Semblov!" said another.

"Murder! Murder in the streets of Bobbin!" said a third.

Zenith dropped the knife and bolted from Semblov's stall, sprinting through the narrow lane, down stone steps, and across a wider passageway. He climbed a longer set of steps, darted across a courtyard, and climbed again. He encountered little level ground and many steps, most of them leading up. It was as if the city had been designed by a sadistic gym teacher, or perhaps the architect of Eternity Tower.

Zenith paused to catch his breath and rub his

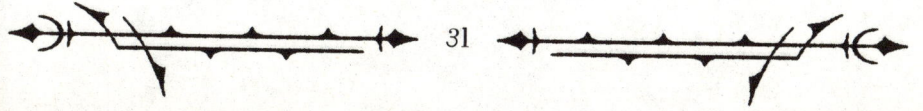

sore feet, regretting his decision to jettison his shoes in the Scalding Sea. The sound of the pursuing mob grew louder. He scanned the abandoned courtyard around him.

And found a human-looking man beckoning from a shadowed alcove. Zenith, both curious and frantic, stepped toward the stranger. With surprising strength, the bearded old man grasped Zenith's shirt, yanked him into the darkened recess, and clasped a bony hand over his mouth.

A moment later, the townsfolk stormed through the courtyard and up the next set of steps. The old man held Zenith tightly till their voices faded. Releasing the boy, he laughed congenially. "Sorry to be rough, but there was no time to discuss."

Zenith backed away. "Uh, no problem." He scratched his scar nervously. Outside of Apogee and Kevin, Zenith had never encountered another seemingly human creature in GrahBhag. He said, "Who or what are you?"

The old man chuckled. "Firman, of course, like you. Very much like you. I'm your great-grandson."

Grandpa

"**YOU'RE MY WHAT?**" said Zenith.

"I'm your great-grandson," said the old man. He frowned. "Or am I your great-grand*father*? Ugh! Time travel is so confusing. Never mind. Come with me." He ambled across the courtyard, and Zenith followed, caution overshadowed by curiosity. "Schrödinger will straighten the whole thing out."

The man guided Zenith through a network of concealed passageways to the back of an isolated building.

"Be it ever so humble," said the old man as he ushered Zenith inside a musty, windowless apartment. "Schrödinger? Where are you?"

From somewhere nearby, a youthful, feminine voice replied, "You know where I am, Grandpa P. I'm always in the same place."

"Of course, my dear." The old man led Zenith

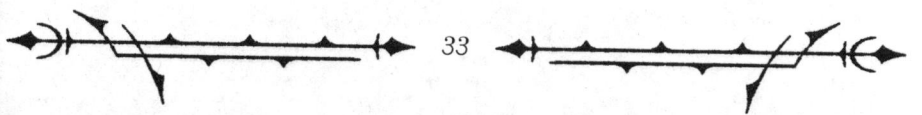

around an overstuffed sofa to a humble kitchen nook with a wooden table and two mismatched chairs. Atop the table was a square silver-tone metal box, perhaps nine inches deep. Its hinged lid was open, and a kitten sat inside. Her fur was black with tiny white speckles, reminding Zenith of the midnight sky. "This is Schrödinger," said the old man, giving the cat a pat on the head. "Schrödinger, this is my great-grandson. Or great-grandfather?" He shook his head and shuffled through a nearby doorway. "You'll know better than I."

The kitten offered Zenith one fluffy forepaw. "I'm Schrödinger's *Cat*, actually. Not Schrödinger. Explained it to him a million times, but he can't keep anything straight. Forget all that nonsense about you two being related. He thinks he's related to everyone. It's just who he is."

"And that would be . . . ?" asked Zenith.

"He's called Grandfather Paradox." The kitten's ears perked up. She yowled, "Duck!"

The old man reappeared in the doorway and hurled a dagger at Zenith. The boy ducked as it whizzed past his head and stuck in the wall behind him where the plaster was pockmarked with other blade-shaped incisions. The old man shuffled quickly across the room, toward the knife. "Travel back in time to kill me, will you? We'll see who ends up dead."

"No one's trying to kill you, Grandpa. Now, come sit down," said the cat. "You're being rude."

"Yes, my dear." The old man reversed direction, sat at the table, and smiled pleasantly at Zenith, who took the other chair, sitting as far from his would-be assassin as possible.

The cat turned to Zenith. "Sorry about that. His whole existence is based on the idea that his descendant will travel back in time to kill him. But if the descendant kills Grandpa P before Grandpa P can father the descendant's parent, then the descendant would never exist, and therefore *couldn't* travel back to kill their grandfather in the first place. Deep down, Grandpa P knows it's all a logical impossibility, and it muddles his mind." She licked her paw and cleaned her ear. "But that's what you get when you bring abstract theories to life."

Zenith said, "When who does what?"

The cat said, "Him. Me. We're both abstract theories brought to life by the Scribe, using the Firman craft of science."

"Science?" An image from his last GrahBhagian adventure popped into Zenith's head—a textbook winging its way across the sky like a bird, flying toward the Collectory. "Are you saying Muncie has my sister's physics book?"

The cat perked up. "*Your* sister's physics book?" She gave him a sniff. "Can it be? Are you Zenith Maelstrom?"

Zenith looked at the dagger stuck in the wall. Would Grandpa P use it again if Zenith admitted who he was? He gave the old man a long look, then, swallowing hard, Zenith showed the cat the A-shaped scar on his wrist. "I am."

The cat gasped. "You *are*." She purred loudly. "How long I've prepared for this day!" She looked at the old man. "We're saved!"

"Happy you're happy," said Zenith with relief. "But how are you saved, and from what?"

"Things have gone downhill since you left. The Scribe did capture your sister's book. He was smitten with its contents and began integrating its scientific principles into the Collectory." The kitten shuddered. "It's a dangerous mix of magics that is destabilizing GrahBhag and threatening its very existen—"

The old man shut the box's lid abruptly. "Hush now, Schrödinger. All your jibber-jabber makes my head hurt."

Zenith scowled at Grandfather Paradox and opened the box. The kitten lay limp, apparently knocked out. Zenith leaned forward, gave the cat a sniff, then recoiled. "She's . . . dead. How is she dead?"

Grandfather Paradox chuckled and said, "Don't worry about Schrödinger. She's got nine lives and then some." He closed the lid again and immediately reopened it.

The cat sprang up like a jack-in-the-box and clutched at Zenith's shirt with her claws. "Don't let Grandpa P close my lid again! There's no telling what'll happ—"

The old man shut it once more. "Nap time." He walked to the dagger in the wall. "I'll be in my bedroom." He yanked the knife free and pointed it at Zenith. "Snuggling with my little lifesaver here, in case you get any homicidal notions." As Grandpa retreated, Zenith lifted the box lid slightly. The stench curled his nostril hairs. "Hey, now." The old man waved the knife. "You let Schrödinger get her catnap. And you bunk on the couch."

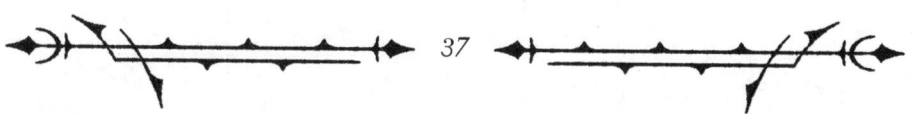

Grandfather Paradox watched Zenith back away from the box to the sofa. Zenith sat still as the old man closed and locked the door.

Only after Zenith heard loud snoring did he tiptoe back to the table. Feeling like a magician who hadn't mastered a trick, he repeatedly opened and closed the box's lid. The third time wasn't the charm, nor was number seven lucky. Thirteen remained cursed, and sixteen was not so sweet. The cat stubbornly remained dead.

He was about to give up when Schrödinger's Cat was finally resurrected. She peeked above the box's edge and whispered, "Where's Grandpa P?"

"Sleeping," whispered Zenith.

The cat pointed one paw at the front door. "Let's get out of here."

Zenith picked up the box and tiptoed across the wood floor, grateful to be in stocking feet and to be leaving the muddled, murderous old man behind.

Barter and Banter

ZENITH'S GRATITUDE LASTED until he opened the door. Seeing the uneven cobblestone path, he wished for two things—a pair of shoes for his aching feet and anonymity. He briefly recounted the events at Semblov's stall and wondered if the cat was acquainted with the network of tunnels the old man had taken him through.

Schrödinger's Cat said, "Don't fret. Grandpa P isn't the only one taking a nap. All of Bobbin enjoys an afternoon rest each day. The streets will be empty for the next hour. More than enough time for us to leave town. The thing to worry about is keeping my lid open."

"And shoes," said Zenith. "If I could 'borrow' a pair of shoes, that would be great."

The cat guided him to a nearby bazaar, where vendors' merchandise had been left unattended during

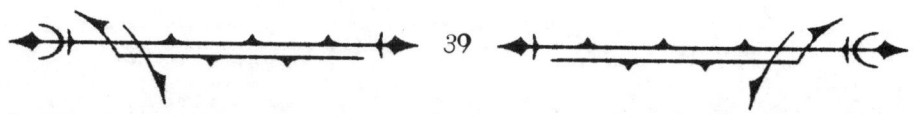

the siesta. Thievery was exceedingly rare in Bobbin, as the penalty for theft was a severed hand. The cat suggested a trade would be the safer, more honorable choice. Firman goods were both unique and valuable, so Zenith left his sea-stained T-shirt, and in exchange gained an ensemble of GrahBhagian apparel: a pair of boots, a long-sleeve tunic, and an expansive scarf to wrap around his head and hide his infamous face. Zenith would've gladly traded in his soggy socks, the bottoms of which were now a grimy blue-green, but he couldn't find any replacements.

As they started up another of Bobbin's numerous stairways, Zenith said, "So, you were saying, everyone's doomed..."

"Yes." The cat's ears drew back. "Unfortunately, the Scribe took a scattershot approach to his scientific 'enhancement' of the Collectory, flipping through your sister's book and transcribing whichever passages caught his fancy. He was particularly taken with the chapter on quantum physics.

"New creatures were born from quantum theories. The entire countryside was infested with quarks, strange little things constantly jockeying for position among themselves, though some of them were

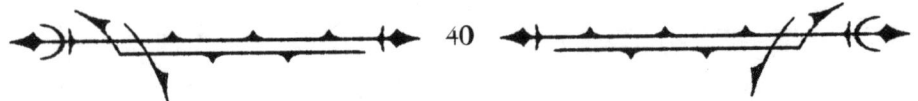

quite charming. A simple spelling error created the Uncertainty Principal, an absentminded headmaster who constantly searched for students to lecture, but became unsure of what to say when anyone stopped to listen.

"Grandpa P and I were created the same way. Though the Scribe made me, I owe my life to that lovable kook. There's no telling how long I sat dead inside this box or how many times Grandpa P opened it before I was alive."

Zenith said, "My science teacher mentioned Schrödinger's Cat this past year. The point is that the cat—I mean, you—might be poisoned, but when the box is closed, there's no telling whether you're alive or dead, so you're both, theoretically speaking. But you're alive right now, so why don't you hop out of the box before you end up dead again?"

The cat growled fearfully. "How could I leave the box? We are one thought experiment, born together and inseparable. It was painful enough leaving Grandpa P behind. But it will be worth it if we're able to save GrahBhag."

Zenith said, "Nothing you've described seems cataclysmic."

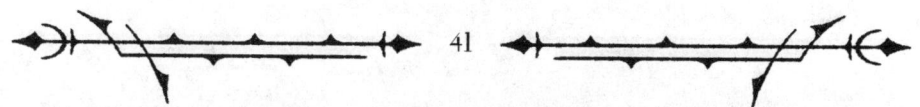

"If the Scribe had stuck to the creation of delightful creatures like me, no one would be in danger. But recently he added String Theory to the fundamental rules of the Collectory."

Zenith scratched the scar above his ear. "String Theory?"

"As you might suspect, it's not an elegant manifestation of your scientific theory, but a fragmentary distortion. Your physicists have posited that all matter is made of infinitesimal strings, and when these strings vibrate, they create the fundamental building blocks of the universe. But the Scribe has conflated the strings of String Theory with the threads holding GrahBhag together. And when the GrahBhagian threads vibrate, they throw those elementary forces into disarray and destabilize the connections between the Eleven Realms."

Schrödinger's Cat paused expectantly. Zenith said, "Could you slow down and circle back to the phrase 'String Theory' for a minute?"

"Oh, close my lid," said the cat. "You have no idea what I'm talking about, do you?"

"Not the slightest."

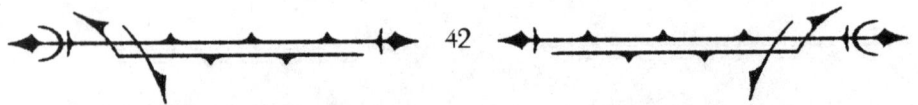

"But you brought the Firman book of science to GrahBhag!"

"Yeah, but it's my sister's book. She's read more of it than I have."

"So the Poison One is the master of science?"

"No. Forget all you've heard about the 'Poison One' and the 'Dread Outlaw Maelstrom.' We're just two kids who got in over our heads and were lucky enough to survive. At least, I *hope* my sister survived."

The cat emitted an amused meow. "Number one on the Royal Guard's most wanted list? She's very much alive."

Zenith exhaled with relief. He was finally back in GrahBhag, and it was even more treacherous than before. But he would gladly endure as many deadly trials as necessary for the chance to save Kevin and Apogee. "Do you know where she is?"

"No. She keeps herself well hidden, lest the Wraith or Its loyal forces find her. Her whereabouts are unknown."

"I might be able to solve the mystery." For the first time since his hectic return to GrahBhag, Zenith tried to use his special insight to locate his sister. Knowledge of her whereabouts had been granted when he'd written his message on the Collectory's enchanted chalkboard. He'd been unable to flex this mental muscle during their interworld separation, and now he couldn't generate anything more than a momentary flicker in his mind's eye. Apparently the power had grown weak with disuse.

"Are you in pain?" asked the cat. "Why are you straining so?"

Zenith gave up and said, "It's nothing. I'm fine," but he was badly shaken by his failure. How was he ever going to find Apogee?

Struggles

BOBBIN'S MANY STEPS gave way to a rocky trail leading to the top of the sea cliff. Zenith paused and looked back at the city clinging to the rock face below. Before them, no more than fifty yards away, was the edge of a forest with a dozen different species of trees, entangled and entwined.

Zenith looked to the cat. "Is that Whichway Woods?"

"Yes. Why?"

"I'm hoping my friend Kevin is there." He moved briskly toward a stitched seam running along the leathery terrain. "I'm bringing him back home along with my sister."

"Stay away from those stitches," said the cat. "As I said, String Theory has—oh, right. You have no idea what I'm saying and no clue how to solve

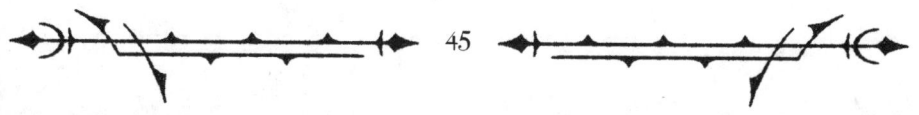

GrahBhag's crisis. I might as well close my lid and hope for another death."

"Hey, we have earthquakes back home. I don't need to understand why they happen to know they're bad news. The portal I used to get here vanished right before my eyes. There was a tremor and this painful, musical sound."

"Yes." The kitten began to purr. "That's what I've been talking about. Maybe you're right. I've studied the theory, and you've had the field experience. Perhaps together we can save GrahBhag."

"Whoa. I didn't say anything about saving GrahBhag. I came here to get my sister and best friend and go back home."

The cat's ears flattened against her head. "And how exactly will you do that, Zenith Maelstrom? Your portal to Terra Firmament has disappeared. Maybe you'll find another, maybe not. If so, what might follow you home? The current interdimensional chaos has brought several alien entities to my world. Why would yours be any different?"

Zenith didn't have an answer. Actually, he did have an answer, and it was "it won't be," but he didn't want to say that aloud. Instead, he mumbled, "I need

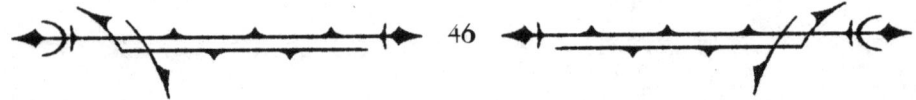

to focus on the trail." Silence descended as they were swallowed by the forest's shadows.

While he battled the foliage trying to ensnare him, Zenith struggled with his thoughts as well. Ever since he'd been forcibly ejected from GrahBhag, he'd been frantic to return. When the opportunity arose, he'd jumped blindly without any plan, figuring his instincts and wits would serve him as well as they had in the past.

But now his instincts and wits were at war. His first impulse was to grab Kevin and Apogee and run home. But how? He'd entertained some vague notion he'd force Stickyfingers to dissolve the glue she'd used to seal the hilltop's portals. But were the foul mouths still there? Or were they now traveling around the cosmos like their cousin Salty?

And if GrahBhag was left in such an unstable state, what might come to Earth? He pictured a multunus swamping ships on the high seas. He imagined GrahBhagian creatures swarming the streets of his hometown, hunting prey to frighten and feast upon. He saw the Wraith hovering above Apogee's bed, poised to smother her in its toxic embrace. He couldn't dismiss these fantasies as far-fetched. But

should the burden to fix things fall on his eleven-year-old shoulders?

The cat interrupted his tumultuous thoughts with a low growl. "Maelstrom, watch where you step."

Zenith stopped and looked down. Beneath the moss, the ground bore a stitched seam the color of tree sap. It began vibrating.

"Get away." The kitten cowered in her box. "Now!"

The ground rolled gently, then lurched violently. Zenith fell to his knees. He dropped the cat's box and covered his ears as they were assaulted by a strident musical tone. Large gaps in the seam began to form, and a sour gas billowed out, burning his throat.

The earsplitting sound ceased, and the shaking stopped. Zenith grabbed the cat in the box, scooted away from the fissures, and braced for whatever otherworldly beast might emerge.

Fouler Mouths

WHAT CAME FROM the larger opening was the voice of Little Mouth. She sounded phlegmy and fatigued, as though she'd been battling a respiratory infection. "Unhappy to see you again, Firman fool."

The smaller gap coughed, then said, "Zenith Maelstrom is not the source of our suffering." It was the raspy voice of Dry Mouth.

Zenith said, "What're you two doing here? And where's your big sister?"

Sounding queasy, Little said, "Your moronic questions never cease."

"I guess it doesn't matter why you're here," said Zenith, drawing nearer. "If I can find Apogee and Kevin, we can all go home."

"Stay back, Zenith," said Dry. "It's not safe to get close."

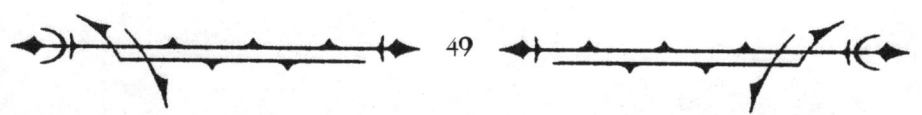

"Why?"

Little Mouth exploded like a miniature volcano, expelling a viscous green effluvium that blanketed the nearest bushes, instantly reducing them to ash. Zenith felt a sudden flash of heat as a dollop of glop burned a hole straight through the tip of his boot. Luckily the GrahBhagian footwear was a bit large, and his toes were unharmed.

Zenith stepped back. "Okay, that's why."

Dry Mouth said, "We no longer connect to Terra Firmament. The links between worlds have gone—" The mouth closed tightly, then burst open and vomited corrosive slime onto a nearby tree, leaving a softball-size hole in its trunk.

"Haywire," said Zenith.

"We now connect GrahBhag with Gausia," said Dry Mouth. "An inhospitable world of lava, bile, acid, and other vile substances."

"You'd feel right at home," said Little Mouth. "Time there moves as slowly as your dull brain. Happy to send you there for free." She released a light liquid spray and a sulfuric stench.

"No thanks." Clutching the cat's box, he hustled away. "Best of luck. Hope you find your sister."

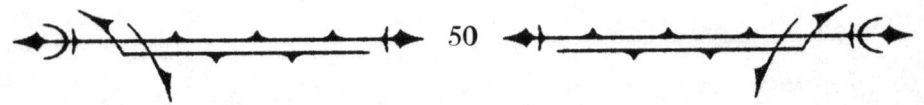

As they fled from the foul mouths, Zenith fell silent once again. *Missing sister—I've got one too.* He vacillated between a paper-thin optimism and a deep sense of doom. There was still a slim chance of escape. If he could find Apogee. If Big Mouth remained on the hilltop, unaffected by the String Theory quake that had repositioned her sisters. But it was more likely she'd become disconnected from Earth and linked to some alien hellscape. Then again, things had looked hopeless before and he and Apogee had always found a way out. Actually, Apogee had elected to stay in GrahBhag and had *kicked* Zenith out. Who was to say she would be happy to see him reappear?

Zenith's thoughts went round, retracing the same mental steps.

"Why are we retracing the same steps?" asked the cat.

"Are we?" Apparently, Zenith was lost physically as well as mentally. Nothing around him seemed familiar. And why should it? During his previous trips, Kreeble had guided him through this hostile forest. Why had he thought he'd be able to navigate it on his own?

The cat whispered, "I think we're being followed."

The skin on the back of Zenith's neck prickled as he realized she was right. His sore feet were on the stone path, so the crunching of underbrush wasn't coming from him. Neither was the ragged breathing or rank odor. An unseen something was tracking them. Unlike the somethings from that first frightful night in Whichway Woods with Apogee, this creature might not be content to merely watch.

He gently set the cat's box down in the middle of the footpath, tiptoed toward the source of the sounds, and peered through a tall bush's branches.

A pair of bloodshot eyes stared back.

Zenith shrieked. The creature yowled. Zenith grabbed its shabby garment, pulling them both off balance. They tumbled to the ground, and Zenith ended up on top. He straddled the beast's belly and pinned its grimy wrists to stop it from raking him with its claws. It squirmed impotently. Zenith scowled at its filthy face, then leaned in closer.

"Kevin?"

Reunion

KEVIN SHUT HIS eyes and twisted his shoulders, almost breaking Zenith's grip on his wrists.

Zenith tightened his hold. "Kevin, open your eyes. It's me. Zenith."

His friend refused to look at him. "Sister, help! A fleshy warlock is stealing my brain-holdings. He has taken my name, but I will keep yours safe. I swear it, dear Kreeble."

"Kreeble?" Zenith leaned in close again. "Did you say 'Kreeble'?"

Kevin stopped struggling. "All right, wizard," he sighed. "Plunder my mind. I am powerless to stop you. But leave the rest of my kinfolk alone."

"Do not despair, brother," said Kreeble as she crept out of a nearby bush. "This is an old friend of the family."

Zenith released Kevin, who ran to the gargoyle,

trying to hide behind the much smaller creature. Zenith wished Kevin *was* hidden, because the sight of him was painful. His clothes were grimy and torn. He was caked with mud and leaves from head to toe. And the state of those toes! Grubby and calloused, with toenails so long they curled down to the ground. His fingernails were more conservative in length, but sharper. Zenith noted the leaves covering his clothes and body mimicked the pattern of Kreeble's scales. His sludge-encrusted hair was styled to copy her spikes.

Kreeble whispered to Kevin, who then ran into the forest. Before Zenith could object, Kreeble said, "I have sent Kevin ahead to inform Kribble, Krobble, and Krone of your return. They shall prepare a meal for our arrival."

Zenith shook his head. "What is going on?"

Kreeble scurried up to her old place on Zenith's shoulder. "The first of many questions, I am sure. I will answer them. But first . . ." The gargoyle scooped a fingerful of wax from Zenith's right ear, tasted it, and sighed. "Delicious. Oh, how I have missed your grits!"

"Feel free to talk with your mouth full and tell

me what happened to Kevin." Zenith picked up Schrödinger's Cat, nestled in her box.

Kreeble prodded his shoulder with her heel. "Walk while we talk, or we shall never get home." Zenith began walking, and she said, "You must be shocked by Kevin's transformation. Rest assured, he undertook these changes voluntarily, out of a desire to fit in with his family."

"Why would a human boy think a bunch of gargoyles are his family?"

"Because Kevin has no idea he is human."

Zenith stopped in his tracks. "What?"

This time, Kreeble kicked him and said, "I know you are easily confused, but please minimize nonsensical exclamations. Kevin was shut off from your world, as you are well aware. Kribble, Krobble, Krone, and I looked after him in our crypt. After recovering from the Wraith's attack, Kevin went about exploring Whichway Woods, hoping to make the most of his 'vacation' before you returned. When Kribble brought news that your sister had remained in GrahBhag, Kevin tried unsuccessfully to find her.

"But days became weeks, and Kevin's boundless

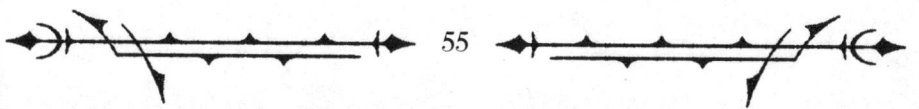

energy faded. As the weather grew colder, he stayed closer to the crypt, which he started calling 'home.' He spoke of his Firman home less and less. During winter hibernation, gargoyles spend three-quarters of each day in a deep stone sleep. Kevin was alone for many hours.

"One morning upon waking, Kribble found Kevin climbing the stairs. Kribble blocked his exit and asked the boy what he was doing. Kevin's answer made it clear he remembered nothing about Terra Firmament or his former life. He only knew he was different from us. He wanted to find where he belonged.

"The GrahBhagian winter might have killed Kevin. To keep him with us, Kribble insisted he was indeed a member of our gargoyle family, one who had been born special: larger, without the usual layer of scales, and suffering from a mild case of stonebrain, which had calcified his memory."

Zenith said, "Why not tell him the truth?"

"About an unseen, unreachable world of which he had no recollection?"

Zenith recalled how, after he and Apogee were safely back home, he had repeatedly forgotten

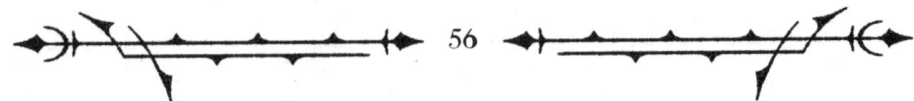

everything about their first adventure in GrahBhag. Some supernatural power erased human knowledge of other worlds, and apparently it was at work in GrahBhag as well as on Earth.

Kreeble said, "Kevin accepted Kribble's story and set about learning how to be a proper gargoyle. Krone tutored him in our history. Kribble relayed current events. I showed him how to forage, and Krobble taught him how to climb—and fight—the toughest trees in the forest. Despite his anxious behavior just now, Kevin is generally happy."

Thinking of his muck-covered friend, Zenith doubted the past two GrahBhagian years had been good for Kevin. But he understood the gargoyles had been generous and kind. "Thanks, Kreeble. I know you did your best in an impossible situation."

Now Zenith was faced with his own impossible situation. Cleaning up Kevin would be simple. And perhaps he'd find some way to revive his memory. But there was one aspect of Kevin's transformation Zenith was powerless to undo. Even hunched over, it was clear Kevin had grown several inches. Eleven-year-old Kevin had been a husky kid. But thirteen-year-old Kevin, aged preternaturally by

GrahBhagian time, was tall, gangly, and undernourished. Would Zenith's now six-year-old sister have changed as radically?

If they ever managed to get home, how could Zenith explain the others' unearthly metamorphoses?

Fireside Chat

BACK AT THE gargoyles' catacomb home, the group ate silently. They sat around a fire built amid the ruins of an ancient sarcophagus. Zenith felt a bit queasy. He'd always thought the jagged stone remnants seemed the result of violence rather than age and decay.

His unease was amplified by the sight of his old friend sitting on the opposite side of the circle. Kevin noticed Zenith's attention and shrank down behind Krobble's broad shoulders.

Schrödinger's Cat cleared her throat. "This fish is quite delicious."

Kribble said a little too loudly, "Kevin taught us how to catch them."

Kevin lifted his head. "I did? I do not remember that."

Krobble patted his hand. "We know you do not, dear heart."

"Zenith Maelstrom," scolded Krone. "Stop staring and move your mouth. Use it to eat or speak. I care not which."

Zenith did both simultaneously, cramming some fish in his mouth while mumbling, "Sorry," which splooched the half-chewed food back onto his plate. "I'm a bit overwhelmed being back in GrahBhag and seeing all the . . . changes."

Kreeble shook her head. "I doubt you have seen all that has changed, unless you have done the impossible and located your sister."

"You said you couldn't find her after I got tossed out. Is she always hidden?"

Kribble said, "On the contrary. The Warrior Witch and her band of rebels appear out of thin air to strike terror into the hearts of evildoers and fight for the liberation of the oppressed."

Krone waved her hand at the younger gargoyle dismissively. "As you can see, Kribble has become a fan of your sister. He is not alone. Her group's daring battles against the Royal Guard have endeared her to much of the populace."

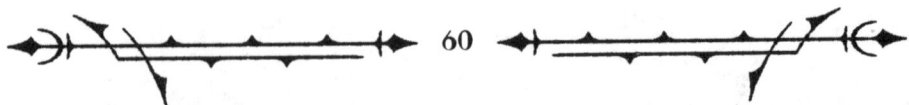

"Related to the Warrior Witch, is he?" Kevin whispered to Krobble. "Knew he was a warlock."

Kreeble said, "Much of Apogee's activity has centered on gaining access to the Collectory."

Zenith leaned forward. "Has she changed her age again?"

"No. Her forays have been unsuccessful," said Kreeble. "And now there is a large contingent of the Royal Guard permanently stationed at the Collectory."

Krone said, "The clerics declared the Scribe's experiments with Firman science counter to the best interests of GrahBhag. They brought in the Guard and redirected the Scribe's efforts."

"Rumor has it," said Kribble, "they are attempting to change the Wraith back into the Great and Holey Wurm."

Zenith held his scarred wrist close to his chest. The firelight took on the shape of the red-cloaked demon as images of its various attacks flooded his mind. He looked at Krone. "Could the Collectory do that?" He looked at Schrödinger's Cat. "Could quantum physics do that?"

The cat said, "I'm not sure."

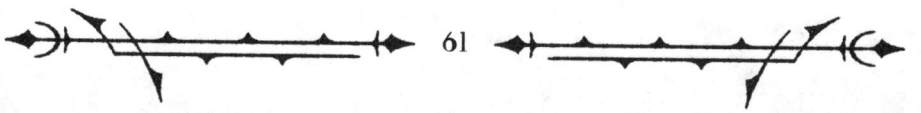

Krone shrugged. "They have not done it yet. The Wraith still haunts the countryside, hunting for your sister. The Royal Guard also pursues her. But neither has discovered her hideout."

Zenith had hoped the gargoyles would supply some clue to Apogee's location. Briefly, he tried again to summon his special power. Was the flicker in his mind's eye a bit brighter? Sounding more confident than he felt, he declared, "With your help, I'll find Apogee. We'll start the search tomorrow."

16

Sleep Over

THE YOUNGER GARGOYLES bedded down around the dying fire alongside Zenith. Schrödinger's Cat asked to be placed farther away, as her metal box had overheated during their meal. After assurances from Krone that they would all be safe sleeping next to a warlock, Kevin nestled among the gargoyles.

Zenith's GrahBhagian scarf served as a pillow, alleviating the physical discomfort of the stone floor. But his mental distress kept him awake long after the others had fallen asleep. Even Kevin, who'd kept one suspicious eye trained on Zenith, had succumbed and started to snore.

The silly, obnoxious sound reminded Zenith of a sleepover he'd had with Kevin in the Churls' backyard six Earth weeks ago. Kevin had smuggled a huge bag of gummy worms inside his sleeping bag. The boys gorged on half, then used the remainder for a boisterous food fight. After a semiserious scolding from Mr. Churl, the boys shifted to whispered conversation. They'd vowed to stay up all night, but before long, Kevin fell asleep and began his ridiculous snoring.

Now Zenith vowed to heal his damaged friend. But rehabilitating Kevin was just one of the challenges before him. He also needed to locate Apogee, convince her to leave, and find a way home for all of them. How could he possibly add saving horrible GrahBhag to this already overwhelming list?

Zenith tossed and turned, frustrated by his restless mind, but at the same time hopeful that his anxiety would activate his special power and produce a dream that revealed Apogee's whereabouts, as it had during his last visit to GrahBhag.

When he finally fell asleep, it did just that. But the images were dark and fragmentary, as if Apogee was also having a restless night. When Zenith awoke the next morning, he kept his eyes closed, struggling to hold on to the fragile imagery.

A snorting laugh made him open his eyes. Kevin

was looming over him. "You make silly faces when you sleep." He scrambled on all fours across the crypt and up the stairwell, snorting all the way.

Gratitude and frustration flared inside Zenith. He was thankful Kevin was warming up to him, but also irritated by Kevin's bad timing. All traces of the dream had vanished. Zenith rose stiffly off the floor and slowly climbed the steps, his feet aching worse than they had the day before.

Everyone was gathered for breakfast. Schrödinger's Cat gnawed on another roasted fish. The four gargoyles and Kevin hunched over a wooden bowl. Kreeble said, "Your troubled expression suggests the reception of bad news. Did the casket beetles speak to you? Do not believe a word they say."

"Not bad news, no news," said Zenith. "I was hoping my dreams would provide a clue to Apogee's location, but I can't remember anything."

"Perhaps something will come back to you." Kreeble offered him her place. "Meanwhile, eat."

Kevin wiggled his green-tinted fingers at Zenith. "The root slime is tasty today." He stuck all five fingers in his mouth.

Zenith's stomach did a somersault. "Um, maybe

a little later." He glanced at the contents of the gargoyles' bowl, his eyes widening.

"See something you like?" asked Krobble.

"Yes, I do," said Zenith. The fungi in the bowl had brought back something from his dream. "Does a giant blue mushroom with tiny red dots mean anything to you?"

The gargoyles exchanged a worried look. Kribble whispered, "Only doom and despair."

Krone said, "Such mushrooms grow in Canker Grove, the oldest part of Whichway Woods. The plant life is ancient and deadly. Those who stray there almost never return."

A Ticklish Situation

ZENITH SAT ON a stump and wolfed down some roast fish, fueling up for the trip to Canker Grove. After failing to dissuade him, Kribble, Krobble, Krone, and Kevin had returned to the catacombs, but Kreeble wasn't done trying.

"Did you not hear Krone? She used the Anglish word 'deadly.' As in 'death.' As in 'death is waiting for you in Canker Grove.'"

Zenith wiped his mouth on his wrist. "No, what she said was *almost* no one comes back. That means some do."

Kreeble crossed her arms. "What makes you think you will be among those lucky few? With no one there beside you?"

Schrödinger's Cat raised her paw. "I'll be there. And I face death every day."

"As I understand it," said Kreeble, "you cannot

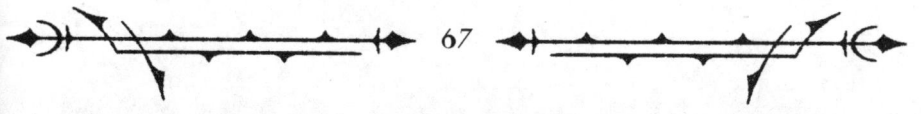

leave your box-home. Plus, you are small, and your claws are quite short."

Zenith nudged Kreeble. "Your claws are long, and you know how to use them. C'mon, let's make a deal. There must be some disgusting body junk I can trade in exchange for your help."

"None of your grits are worth the risks associated with such an expedition."

Krobble exited the crypt, carrying Zenith's scarf and boots. She asked Kreeble, "Have you been able to talk him out of his foolhardy plan?"

Zenith took the boots. "Thanks. And no, she hasn't." He tried to slip one on but flinched and dropped it. His feet hurt too much. "What the heck is going on?" He removed both grimy socks and blanched. Covering the pads of his feet and creeping between his toes was a spongy blue-green fungus.

Krobble was stunned. "Kreeble, are you seeing what I am seeing?"

Kreeble was wide-eyed. "Yes, Krobble. My line of sight is as clear as your own."

Zenith almost touched the fungus, then stopped himself. "What is this gunk?"

Kreeble and Krobble said, "Sea beast yeast." Their tone was reverential. And ravenous.

"A delicacy derived from microorganisms found in the depths of the Scalding Sea," added Kreeble.

"We have partaken once," said Krobble. "Years ago, when our Uncle Kleet came ashore for a visit."

Kreeble whispered, "It is extremely rare and unspeakably delicious." Her hand drifted toward Zenith's feet.

Which the boy swung skyward, out of the gargoyles' reach. "So which one of you will help me get to Canker Grove in exchange for this yeast feast?"

Krobble stepped forward. "I will!"

"No, it shall be me," said Kreeble, trying to muscle past her more muscular cousin. The gargoyles grappled and growled.

Zenith said, "No need to fight. There's enough of me to go around." He offered one foot to each of them. The gargoyles gripped his ankles as they descended upon his toes. Schrödinger's Cat seemed disturbed, but Zenith couldn't help laughing. His feet were ticklish.

Canker Grove

THEY TRAVELED WITH Krobble in front, Kreeble at the rear, and Zenith in the middle. Schrödinger's Cat rode upon the boy's back, craning her neck and nipping at bugs, real and imagined. Her box was secure within the half-zipped side pocket of Kevin's old duffel bag, which Zenith wore like a backpack. Although Kevin had long ago consumed the bag's stash of snack bars, the most important item had remained waiting inside—the semisentient baseball bat. This bat had come in handy during Zenith's last trip, when he'd used it to send the Wraith flying into an enormous patch of snagweed.

Now the sports-weapon hummed with satisfaction as Zenith used it to beat back encroaching branches and slithering roots, the bat's need to strike things fulfilled. The gargoyles bushwhacked barehanded, having transformed their arms into stone up to their elbows. Krobble's hands were fixed into fists, and Kreeble's fingers splayed open, claws extended.

The farther they went, the denser and darker the woods became. The botanical assaults intensified. And Zenith's psychic sense of Apogee's whereabouts grew stronger. He knew they were heading in the right direction.

Schrödinger's Cat asked, "How are your feet holding up?"

"Fine," said Zenith. "Krone's salve has done wonders, though most of the pain was eliminated with the yeast. Kreeble and Krobble were very thorough."

"Indeed."

They approached a patch of barren land on the far side of which was a grove of trees, ancient and diseased. Their enormous gray trunks were covered in blistered, blighted bark. Mustard-colored sap oozed from numerous hollows, adding a sickly-sweet aroma to the humid air. All manner of fungus sprang forth from their shallow root systems. A gargantuan network of thick, thorn-covered vines ran amid the primeval thicket, blocking their way.

"Snagweed," said Krobble.

"Much larger than any I have ever seen," said Kreeble.

"And much nastier, I'm guessing," added Zenith. He kicked the dusty ground. "But I *know* Apogee is on the other side of it."

Krobble shook her head. "We cannot fight our way through."

"Nor climb over it," said Kreeble.

The vines continued on either side as far as Zenith could see. "And going around will take forever."

"There's another problem," added the cat, sniffing the air. "Someone is following us."

Krobble took a whiff, then scowled. "Kevin! Where are you?"

"Up here," Kevin said meekly, from atop a nearby tree.

Kreeble crossed her arms. "I thought you were too afraid to come."

"I was. But then I was more afraid of missing out."

A tendril of snagweed shot across the clearing, snapping a sizable branch from the tree and toppling Kevin to the ground. The same tendril ensnared Kevin's ankles, then yanked him back toward

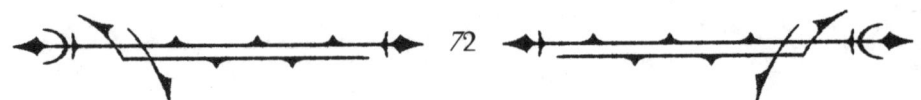

the snagweed patch's dark tangles. Zenith, Kreeble, and Krobble ran after Kevin and were just as easily captured. Suddenly Zenith found himself hanging upside down, his wrists and ankles bound by vines. Another tendril of snagweed displaying an enormous blossom snaked toward his face, petals spreading to reveal several rows of gleaming teeth.

Vine Tamer

THE BLOSSOM HALTED short of Zenith's face. Its tonguelike stigma vibrated, creating a high-pitched warble. A deep voice warbled in response as a large black-furred beast descended from the branches of a nearby elm. The hulking thing turned to face them. Its fur was merely a hooded cloak, open at the front to reveal a body adorned with patchwork rags and mismatched buttons.

"Albert?" said Kreeble.

"Albert," groaned Zenith. Any hope of salvation evaporated. The question now was whether the eight-foot-tall rag doll, who had twice tried to end Zenith's life in a bizarre effort to "befriend" him, would let the vicious vine kill him or finally do the deed himself. Raggedy Albert removed a small hand ax from his leather belt. Zenith thought, *Yup,*

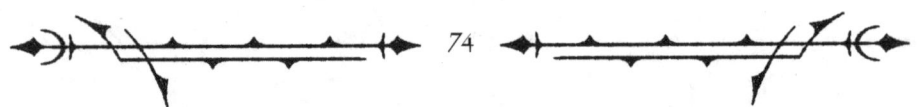

Albert has always been the do-it-yourself type. The rag doll raised his ax above the boy's head.

And sliced through the snagweed, severing Zenith from the bush, though Zenith's wrists and ankles remained bound by the remnants of the vine. Albert lowered Zenith to the ground, then repeated the action with Kreeble, Krobble, and Kevin.

Zenith spotted the bat and the cat's silver box lying on the ground. The bat was inert. The box's lid was closed, so there was no telling whether Schrödinger's Cat was alive or dead.

Albert said, "Rshq vhvdph." The latticework of snagweed vines unraveled and receded before him to create a five-foot-wide opening in the botanical barrier. Albert carried all four captives through at once, depositing them in a rusty wheelbarrow. He tossed the cat's box in as well, but left the bat behind. Albert said, "Forvh vhvdph," and the snagweed barricade re-formed.

The enormous rag doll pushed the cart along a path covered in pine needles and rust-colored leaves. The massive, malignant trees of Canker Grove blotted out the sky, but Raggedy Albert and his prisoners

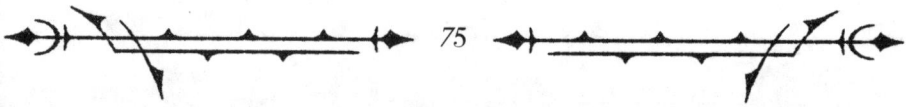

remained unharmed. Zenith gazed up into the giant's button eyes. "All right, Albert, go ahead and make me into one of your taxidermy friends. But leave the others alone."

Albert didn't respond.

Kreeble said, "Perhaps there is a trade to be made. Surely there is something you desire more than Maelstrom's head?"

Again, no reaction.

Kevin asked, "How did you get the snagweed to obey you?"

Albert said, "L'yh fduhg iru wkdw sodqw vlqfh lw zdv d edeb."

Kreeble translated, "He has been cultivating that particular patch of snagweed since it was a seedling."

As the gargoyle understood it, the goliath had disciplined the snagweed with his ax and won its affection by feeding it the innards of the woodland creatures he'd taxidermied. Albert pruned and shaped the snagweed into an impenetrable barrier that protected Canker Grove and gave the area its fierce reputation. Only Albert's allies made it past the wall of ferocious foliage.

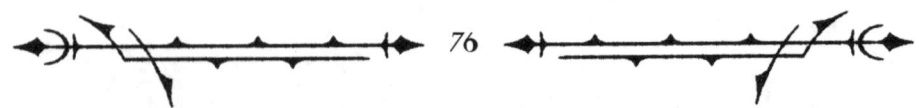

Zenith scoffed. "Since when do you have 'allies' that aren't in the great beyond?"

Albert looked into the distance. "Orqj djr dqg dv ri odwh."

Kreeble said, "Long ago and as of late."

They stopped at a dry riverbed filled with blue mushrooms sporting small red spots and ranging in size from a few inches to several feet tall. None of them were as big as the one from Zenith's dream, but they were clearly the same species. He hoped their appearance meant Apogee was nearby. He felt like she might be.

Albert placed Krobble on top of a large mushroom's wide cap, warbled the same signal as with the snagweed, and said, "Gholyhu." The mushroom tilted till Krobble slid from its cap to the cap of its largest neighbor, which mimicked its action, passing Krobble forward to the next one. Then Kreeble, Kevin, Zenith, and the cat's metal box were all fed onto the fungus conveyor belt. They were passed along, deposited in the mouth of a tunnel, and slid down the smooth rock into a cool, dark cavern.

A brash laugh echoed off the chamber walls, and a voice said, "The others are never going to believe this." A small creature with a humanoid body and the head of a rat loomed over them.

Zenith smiled. "Hello, Loose Lips."

The Hideout

HAVING REMOVED THEIR bindings, Loose Lips led the group through a series of passageways and chambers. More blue mushrooms grew along the cavern walls. Their glowing red spots bathed the cave in crimson light.

Loose Lips's constant chatter was also illuminating. He explained that Raggedy Albert was not just an ax-happy taxidermy enthusiast. He was also a first-rate medic, highly skilled with needle and thread. Albert had fought alongside former Eternity Tower inmate Old Timer years ago, during the failed attempt to stop the Wurm's initial rise to power. They'd retreated to this cavern when the rebellion was crushed, and it was here that Old Timer returned after the escape from Eternity Tower to make things ready for a new generation of rebels.

Since then, those rebels, led by Zenith's little

sister, had conducted daring raids on the clerics' coffers and evaded capture by the Royal Guard numerous times. Loose Lips made it clear that Apogee was considered a brave and clever leader.

The group came to a wondrous grotto, aglow in red light emanating from the blue mushroom Zenith recognized from his dream. Empty sleeping bags were scattered beneath the cap of the massive fungus, behind which garments hung on a clothesline strung between two stalactites. And in the recesses of the chamber, a waterfall spilled into a sparkling pool.

Cleaning cookware at the water's edge was another familiar face. Or more accurately, a familiar eye: a cantaloupe-size, violet eyeball that had once been part of an ocular quartet. Zenith asked Loose Lips, "Is that . . ."

"The last living eyeball of Four Eyes? Yeah. We call it Yellow Eye, because it deserted us during the First Battle for the Collectory. We tolerate the coward because of its connection to the Oracle."

"The what?"

"The Oracle is—No. I've already said too much."

"Come on, Loose Lips."

The rat man spoke low. "Suffice it to say, the Oracle is loyal to the Wraith, but easily misled into doing our bidding."

A group of stool-size toadstools formed a circle around the smoldering campfire. Loose Lips took a seat and gestured for them to join him. He shifted Schrödinger's Cat's box back and forth between his two humanoid hands. "You know, outsiders aren't usually allowed in the Warrior Witch's hideout."

Zenith and Kreeble exchanged glances. "Where *are* Apogee and the others?"

"Out making last-minute prepara—" Loose Lips cut himself off and waved his finger. "Naughty! Trying to make me spill the beans about tomorrow's operation."

"Loose Lips, ye daft idjut," a voice snapped. "Ye just spilled!"

Zenith swiveled around and saw a couple more old acquaintances. The fearsome-looking, boxy-bodied creature who'd scolded Loose Lips was Old Timer. Beside him was another former Tower inmate, Stickyfingers, a lanky being with blue-gray,

porpoise-like skin. Behind them were a scruffy-looking bunch Zenith had never seen before. The members of the group were cloaked in animal pelts, the same as Raggedy Albert.

Old Timer clicked the button on his stopwatch and said, "Ye are pathetic, Loose Lips. Ye run yer fool mouth for ten seconds, and our secrets come tumblin' out."

Zenith said, "That's not fair. He's actually been running his fool mouth for over ten minutes."

Old Timer chuckled. "Good to see ye, yoong Maelstrom. Though yer arrival is ill-timed."

"Yeah, seems like you're pretty busy. Big day tomorrow, huh? Want to tell me more?"

Stickyfingers scrutinized the boys and gargoyles, rubbing her five hands together nervously. "You shouldn't have brought them here, Loose Lips."

The rat man scoffed. "Albert showed them the hideout."

"Enough." A voice echoed from the shadows. A towering figure shrouded in the hide of a lupine beast strode into the light, the pelt's preserved head displaying formidable fangs. Then a small human hand nudged the skull upward. Apogee Maelstrom

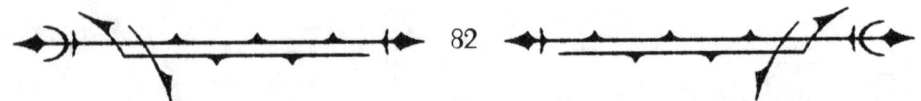

beamed down at Zenith. "This is no way to welcome my brother."

Zenith leapt to his feet. "Apogee!"

The cloak fell to the ground, revealing the little girl astride the broad shoulders of Musclehead, who bent down on one knee. Apogee dismounted and patted the top of his head, barely visible above his extremely overdeveloped musculature. She ran to her brother, hugging him tightly.

Holding his sister, Zenith felt at home for the first time since they were last together. And yet he was overcome with an urgent desire to be truly home, back on Earth, with their parents. He gazed at the face he'd missed so much.

Apogee said, "We've got a lot of catching up to do." She nodded at Old Timer.

Clicking his stopwatch, the old man shouted, "All right, time to eat. Then last checks on yer weapons and off to bed. We leave at daybreak."

Everyone was in motion at once. During the commotion, Zenith stuffed the cat's metal box into his duffel bag.

Apogee's eyes flicked toward Kevin as she asked her brother, "What happened to him?"

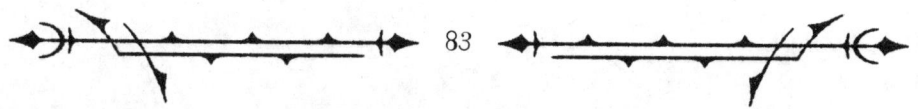

Zenith said, "Besides puberty?" He briefly explained Kevin's amnesia and his belief that he was a gargoyle.

Apogee was silent a moment, then said, "You, Kevin, and the gargoyles come with me."

Plans

APOGEE AND OLD Timer led them under the clothesline and around the curved wall of the cavern. Zenith watched his little sister, a bit confused. The babyish quality her voice had acquired after she'd been regressed to the age of four was gone, but Apogee hadn't grown an inch during Zenith's two-year absence. He hadn't expected her to shoot up like teenage Kevin, but surely she should be bigger.

They came to an area where the rock floor rose up to form a table-like prominence, on top of which were a fountain pen, an inkwell, several sheaves of parchment, and a large quilt. Apogee sorted through the sheaves. "Kevin, come closer, please." She turned the parchment to face him. "Can you tell me what this is?" Before him was a black ink drawing of the horrible bag in all its horrendous glory.

The effect was immediate. Kevin straightened his posture and wiped his eyes as if waking from a dream. Looking down at his muck-and-leaf-covered body, he snorted. Then, turning to Zenith, he said, "How much will I have to pay you to keep this quiet once we're back home?"

Relief washed over Zenith as he laughed. He put his arm around his friend's shoulder. "We'll talk about my price later."

Krobble took a step toward the boys. "You remember your past? You remember Terra Firmament?"

Kevin patted her arm. "I do. And I remember how good you all were to me when I'd forgotten. And everything else since." He put his hands on either side of his head, splayed his fingers, and mimicked the sound of an explosion. "It's like an atomic bomb in there."

Zenith grinned. "Wouldn't an atomic bomb *destroy* everything in there?"

Kreeble gripped Kevin's hand. "Kevin is speaking meta-for-ickly."

"Wow," Zenith said. "We're all learning something today."

Old Timer said, "Come closer. We've got more to teach ye."

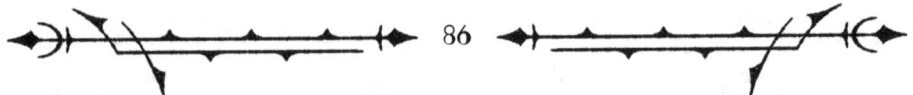

They gathered around the quilt, which was actually a map of GrahBhag. The coverlet was composed of irregularly shaped patches, each representing a distinct geographical region, the boundaries of which were delineated by stitches of different colors and varying thickness.

Old Timer moved color-coded pawns representing the rebels and the various opposing forces around the map as he recapped the rebels' operations. They'd tried invading the Collectory from every direction and with a variety of tactics. But always they were overwhelmed by the Guard's superior numbers. When necessary, the rebels "liberated" fresh supplies from the clerics. But even the simplest-looking raid could turn deadly if the Wraith appeared. The old man plunked a tall red cylinder down in the middle of the pawns, scattering them.

Old Timer placed the rebel pawns on the Whichway Woods patch while recounting the change in their strategy. With a permanent garrison of the Royal Guard now stationed at the Collectory, the rebels turned their energies toward winning the allegiance of the citizenry, with raids designed to enrich the average GrahBhagian rather than themselves.

Their Robin Hood campaign had won them many sympathizers, and the rebels now had a covert network of collaborators in every village.

They would activate that network tomorrow, with planned uprisings across the countryside. With the Royal Guard dispatched to every corner of the map, the Collectory would be defenseless. "And whoever controls the Collectory controls GrahBhag." Old Timer exchanged a satisfied look with Apogee, then turned to their audience. "Well, what do ye think?"

"Sounds reckless," said Zenith. "Count me and my sister out."

Discord

APOGEE BOWED HER head as Old Timer sputtered, "What? With so much at stake, do ye truly plan to abandon us yet again?"

Zenith said, "I hadn't planned on anything, but since you have a full-scale revolution brewing, I don't think it's safe for us three kids to be here."

"But Apogee's our leader."

"So she'll send you all off with a rousing speech and then we can try to find a way home."

"I can't believe it," growled the old man. "Yer a worse coward than Yellow Eye."

Zenith scowled. "Why should I stick my neck out for a place that wants to chop my head off? That's not a metaphor. Your buddy Albert literally tried to sever my head. Twice."

Kevin's voice was quiet but steady. "I'm going to stick *my* neck out."

Zenith was incredulous. "You can't be serious."

"I am. GrahBhag has been my home for two years." He took the gargoyles' hands in his. "I have family here."

Zenith shook his head. "Your home and family are on Earth. Why do you think I came back here?"

"And what about what brought ye to GrahBhag the last time?" asked Old Timer. "Yer sister's proper age needs to be restored."

Zenith laughed. "She's never told you she's supposed to be the 'yoonger' one?"

"If yer sister's wishes mean nothin', what about us? The fate of GrahBhag lies in the balance. The clerics mean to transform the Wraith back into the Wurm and reestablish Its rule. Even if they fail, the Scribe's scientific experiments may tear the world apart."

"My sister and I don't know anything about quantum physics." Zenith pulled the metal box from the duffel bag. "But I have someone who does." He opened the lid.

Everyone gasped.

Kreeble said, "You can see that creature is dead, can you not?"

Zenith cursed his luck and said, "Wait a minute."

As he repeatedly opened and closed the box, Apogee told the others, "Leave us alone, please." When only she and Zenith remained, Apogee gently shut the lid.

Zenith sighed. "Why are we here, Geegee? Why did you ever come to GrahBhag in the first place? Whatever I did to make you change your age, whatever the problem with me being older is, it can't possibly be worth risking your life over."

"Don't you think I want to go back home?" Apogee pushed the stack of parchment toward her brother. Some sheaves were covered with pictures, while others were filled with her bubbly handwriting. Each had a small sketch of the horrible bag in the lower left corner. "I write about our life on Earth every night. But before I can return, I need to find the slate you wrote about us in the Collectory."

"Why? Why can't you just be happy as a six-year-old?"

"Because I'm not a six-year-old," said Apogee, gazing intently into Zenith's eyes. "Two years have passed, and I'm still four."

The Oracle

APOGEE EXPLAINED THAT her age, whether four or fourteen, should've never been specified in writing on the chalkboard, as now it was fixed. It was a silly mistake, one the "all-knowing" Scribe shouldn't have made when he probed Zenith for Details to record. Regardless, the Collectory now proclaimed Apogee was four, and so she would remain until the chalkboard was found and its text revised.

Zenith scratched at the scar above his left ear. It was going to be hard enough explaining teenage Kevin. He had no idea how to sell his parents on eternally four-year-old Apogee. He said, "Geegee, I want you to have a chance at a normal life. But you won't have any sort of life if the Wraith gets you. It seems obsessed with you. Do you have any idea why?"

Apogee squinted as if trying to recall something, but said, "No." Then her face brightened. "Don't worry. Yellow Eye will use the Oracle to lead the Wraith astray before the uprising."

"If you can manipulate It so easily, why not make It drown Itself or set Itself on fire? Destroy It first. *Then* invade the Collectory."

"Too late. The rebellion starts tomorrow. Besides, nobody knows how to destroy the Wraith. And our power over It doesn't work that way." She paused, pursing her lips. "Come on. I'll show you."

They retrieved Old Timer and Yellow Eye from camp, and the group headed around the edge of the shallow pool to the waterfall in the rear of the grotto. They ducked into the gap behind the falling water, entered a narrow passage hidden there, and soon stopped inside a small, candlelit cavern. Apogee whispered briefly to Yellow Eye. Then the eyeball rolled into the next chamber by itself. Old Timer brought Zenith over to this threshold, and whispered, "Be warned. The smell is somethin' fierce." He ducked his head inside and beckoned Zenith to join him.

The odor was indeed shocking. Something was rotting in this confined space. As his watering eyes adjusted to the faint red light emanating from one small mushroom, Zenith understood.

The Oracle, as it was now called, was another eyeball, a decaying doppelganger of Yellow Eye. A broken arrow shaft still protruded from its desiccated sclera, a souvenir of the First Battle for the Collectory. Zenith would've assumed it was dead if not for the Wraith's cryptic symbol swirling at the center of its gray iris. Yellow Eye was snuggled up to its undead sibling, lashes intertwined as in the days when the two of them had been half of Four Eyes's ocular quartet.

Old Timer whispered, "The two can still share thoughts when connected. To prove its loyalty to yer sister, Yellow Eye tells lies to the Oracle. And the Oracle, who is linked to the Wraith mentally even when physically separated, unwittingly passes those lies along to its master. Tomorrow the Wraith will be searching for yer sister far from the Collectory."

Yellow Eye disentangled itself from the Oracle, who seemed to deflate slightly. The symbol in its eye ceased spinning. Old Timer ducked out so Yellow

Eye could pass through, but Zenith lingered behind, sickly fascinated by the corrupted remnant of his former ally. Zenith reached toward the Oracle, his loose sleeve revealing the A-shaped scar on his wrist.

The Oracle jerked to life, eyelashes snaking out and wrapping around the exposed scar. Its touch burned, like the Wraith's. But Zenith's mind was also afire, invaded by a foreign force. A deafening chant arose unbidden inside his head. *Aah Bah Cee, Aah Bah Cee.* And underneath, something fainter wormed its way through the recesses of his mind. The searing heat receded to a comforting warmth, as if the invader were expressing thanks. Then it abandoned him to a cold, indifferent darkness.

Zenith awoke to see Apogee, Old Timer, and Yellow Eye huddled over him. He was back in the candlelit antechamber. He averted his eyes. "I'm sorry."

"What happened in there?" asked Apogee, trying to catch his gaze.

"It got me. The Oracle. The Wraith. It got into my mind."

Yellow Eye rubbed two eyelashes together, creating a few high-pitched squeaks.

"Yes. How?" said Old Timer. "Ye need some sort of connection to either the one or the other."

Zenith pulled his sleeve back, displaying the A-shaped scar.

Apogee said, "So *that's* why you reacted like you did when the Wraith attacked us in Threadbare and Whichway Woods."

"The Wraith gave ye that?" said Old Timer. "That's a major security breach, that is! And what did It find out while It was in that fool head of yers?"

Zenith whispered, "Everything, I think. The plans for tomorrow. The location of this hideout. And how you've been using the Oracle to deceive It."

Old Timer threw up his hands. "That's it. We're done. Once again, Zenith Maelstrom betrays us all!" He plunged back into the narrow tunnel that led back to camp. Yellow Eye rolled behind him.

Zenith kept his eyes on the flickering flame of the candle. "I'm sorry, Apogee."

A large sigh escaped her small body. Apogee said, "I have to tell everyone there's a change of plans." She left without another word.

Although Zenith felt bad about what he'd done, part of him couldn't help but be pleased with the results. With tomorrow's attack canceled, he'd have a chance to figure out some other way to help his sister and get them all home.

Scar Issue

ZENITH EMERGED FROM behind the waterfall to find the camp in commotion. He skirted around the pool and came upon Kevin washing his face by the water's edge. Kevin's ragged clothing lay at his feet, which were newly housed in a pair of sandals. His toenails were trimmed short and neat, as were his fingernails. He wore a tan tunic and matching trousers. When he saw Zenith, Kevin spread his arms and asked, "How do I look?"

Zenith pointed to his hair, which was still filthy and styled to mimic the spikes of a gargoyle. "You missed a spot."

Kevin used a towel to clean his ears. "Oh no, I'm keeping that."

Zenith surveyed the frantic activity. His eyes settled on his sister, who was conferring with Old

Timer from her station atop Musclehead's shoulders. "What's going on?"

Kevin said, "No idea. Been too busy making myself beautiful."

They walked up to Loose Lips, who was draped in the pelt of a wildcat, his head swallowed up within its skull. He stopped cleaning his sword and pointed it at Zenith. "Thanks a lot, blabbermouth. Because of you the attack has been moved up."

"Moved up?" said Zenith. "I thought it was off."

Loose Lips shook his head. "We leave in ten minutes. Got to beat the Wraith to the Collectory." He sheathed his sword and stomped off. "Some people just can't keep a secret!"

A deep, muffled voice said, "And that's why you need to stay behind, Maelstrom." Musclehead marched over, Apogee riding upon his shoulders, cloaked in wolf hide. "Can't have you giving away our every movement to your master."

"The Wraith's not my master," said Zenith. "But I'm happy to stay behind. As long as my sister stays with me."

Apogee looked away. "I can't do that, Nit."

"C'mon, Apogee. I'm sorry I screwed up, but you can't go ahead anyway. Let Old Timer lead the attack while we run away from where the Wraith thinks you're going to be. Because I'm more certain than ever that It's coming for *you*."

Musclehead laughed. "So she should go with Its slave?"

"I'm not Its slave," said Zenith. "What happened with the Oracle was a fluke. I'm not linked to It in any permanent way."

"Then how did the Wraith track us down so quickly in Threadbare and again at the Collectory?" asked Apogee. "Maybe you're more closely connected than you think."

Zenith covered the scar on his wrist. "No."

"There's nowhere to run, Nit. There's nowhere that's safe." Apogee glanced at the cavern. "Including here."

"Thanks to you," said Musclehead as he grabbed both of Zenith's wrists in one meaty fist. "Got to make sure you don't follow us."

"No!" Zenith resisted, but it was like fighting concrete.

Apogee said, "Zenith, please! You're going to hurt yourself."

"Then tell your goon to let go. If I'm a security risk, then so is he. He got hit by the Wraith a lot more than I did."

Musclehead gestured to his bare torso and flexed. "But I'm not marked by It. No scars on me. Now hold still!"

"Hey!" said Kevin. "If we're comparing scars . . ." He lifted his tunic, exposing the multiple distinctive wounds the Wraith had inflicted, all healed but far from invisible. "I think I've got everyone beat."

Magic

"**WHY DID YOU** show them your scars?" asked Zenith. "How does getting yourself tied up alongside me help anyone?"

Kevin said, "You'll see. Once everybody clears out, I'll show you my skills as an escape artist."

"You'll need more than skill to escape," said Stickyfingers, rifling through the duffel bag. Nearby, the two boys sat back-to-back, tied to the same toadstool. "I've coated the ropes holding you in my special secretion. You'd need the claws of a gargoyle to slice through it. Too bad the gargoyles already left for the battle."

"Figures," said Kevin. "I should've never cut my nails."

"We'll send someone back to untie you once the battle is won." Stickyfingers pulled the silver box out of the bag. "What's in here?" She opened the

lid, then slammed it shut. "Oh, no. Why would you carry that around? Poor thing should be buried." She placed the box atop a toadstool. "You two are sick."

As Stickyfingers joined the final stragglers leaving the cavern, Kevin called out, "It's his dead pet, not mine!"

"Worried about your reputation with the people who tied us up?"

"Just wait. They don't call me Magic Kevin for nothing." He twisted his wrists and ankles, trying to loosen their bonds. After minutes of grunting and cursing, Kevin quit. "Okay, maybe they don't call me Magic Kevin. That was useless."

"Oh, I don't know," said Zenith. "I'm pretty sure I just learned some gargoyle swear words."

"There's plenty more where those came from."

"I'm more interested in Raggedy Albert's language right now. There's a word I heard him use that might help us." Zenith paused, recalling the sound, then muttered, "Gooly-hew—No. It was Gholyhoo." He cleared his throat and spoke loudly. "Gholyhoo!"

The mushroom stretched and tilted till the cat's box slid from its cap. The box hit the ground and

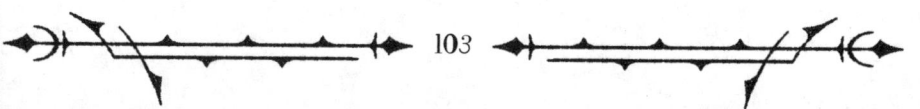

toppled onto its side, causing the lid to fall open. Zenith crossed his fingers.

Schrödinger's Cat's head emerged. "Maelstrom, is that you?"

Kevin elbowed Zenith. "Whoa! Now, that's a magic trick."

Zenith called to the cat. "I need you to come over here and set us free."

The kitten shook her delicate head. "I already told you. I can't leave my box."

"Yes you can. You have to." Zenith continued in a singsong tone, "C'mon. You can do it. C'mon, kitty, kitty, kitty. C'mon, Schrödinger."

The cat hissed and snapped, "Schrödinger's *Cat*! My name is Schrödinger's Cat. And don't patronize me."

Kevin said, "Oh, Schrödinger's Cat. We learned about you in school. That explains the dead/undead thing. I thought you were some sort of zombie cat."

Zenith scowled. "Scaredy-cat's more like it."

"The box and I are a part of the same thought experiment. We belong together," the cat said, hunkering down.

Kevin said, "Hey, isn't there supposed to be a

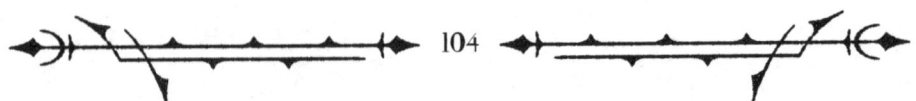

flask of poison, a Geiger counter, and something radioactive in there too?"

"There should be," said the cat. "But the Scribe left them out of his transcription."

"But he wrote that you can't leave the box?" asked Kevin.

"It's never stated outright, just sort of implied," said the kitten, fluffing her tail with her paws.

Kevin shrugged. "That doesn't sound very scientific."

"Wouldn't the scientific approach involve further experimentation?" said Zenith.

The cat lifted her head. "What do you propose?"

In the Tunnels

ZENITH, KEVIN, AND Schrödinger's Cat hurried through an unfamiliar passageway. The "experiments" that had eventually coaxed the cat from her box, one shaky paw at a time, seemed to take forever. Then the newly liberated cat had labored over the secretion-sealed ropes, sawing at them with her claws.

Zenith said, "We've got a lot of ground to make up. Are you sure we're going the right direction?"

"The last sign pointed this way to the Collectory," said Kevin. "Krone taught me how to read GrahBhagian."

"For a shortcut, it doesn't seem very short."

"May not be shorter, but it should be safer. I heard someone say the clerics and Guard don't know about these tunnels."

Schrödinger's Cat said, "Shall I scout ahead?,"

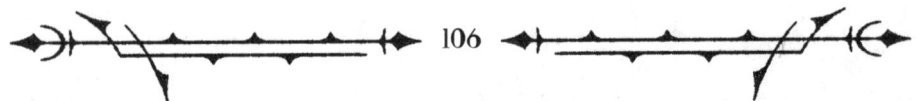

then darted down the passage, disappearing into the shadows.

"She got used to her new freedom quickly," said Kevin, tapping out a rhythm on the side of the cat's metal box. She'd insisted they bring it along but hadn't given it a second glance since.

Zenith yelled, "Schrödinger! Come back."

The cat returned, ears flat. "I've told you—"

"Your name's Schrödinger's Cat, I know," said Zenith. "I just wanted to get you back here. Let's stay together."

The kitten leapt into Kevin's arms and said, "Who's the scaredy-cat now?"

"Me. I'm the scaredy-cat," said Zenith. "I'm afraid we're going to be too late, and the Wraith will get Apogee. I'm afraid the Scribe will turn the Wraith back into the Wurm and then It will get Apogee. I'm afraid that, even if she survives, Apogee's going to be stuck at the age of four forever."

"None of those things are going to happen," said Kevin. "We'll stop the Wraith, fix Apogee's age, and then we'll head home."

Zenith wished he could share Kevin's optimism. But when the Oracle had connected him to the

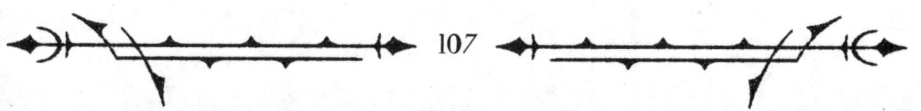

Wraith, Zenith had felt an intense need for Apogee coming from the red specter. He was afraid stopping the Wraith wasn't enough. Even if they changed Apogee's age and made it home, he worried she would never be safe unless the Wraith was destroyed.

They stopped at a junction leading to three separate tunnels. Mushrooms illuminated a sign with arrows and GrahBhagian text.

Kevin translated, "The Collectory is to the right, and still a ways away."

"We're never going to catch them in time," said Zenith, hurrying forward.

Kevin called after him. "Hey! Didn't the slate you wrote give you magical command over Hugh, Seeker of GrahBhag, the fastest creature in the land?"

Turning, Zenith said, "Yeah. So?"

"And didn't you and Kreeble stumble upon the Seeker in a town called Threadbare?"

"Yes. Hugh's favorite pub is there. Why?"

Kevin pointed up. "Because this sign says Threadbare is right above us."

The Rolling Thunder

ZENITH COULD SCARCELY believe their luck. Not only did the short tunnel lead to Threadbare, but it led directly into the storeroom of the Rolling Thunder Tavern. They climbed out of a trapdoor in the floor and found a door opening onto a long hallway. Voices came from the opposite end of the corridor.

With the exception of the stone fireplace and stained-glass windows, the main room was constructed entirely of red oak. A horse-size raven, the Seeker of GrahBhag, was among the handful of customers. Zenith was grateful to see him, but wary. One lucky break was welcome, but two so close together made him nervous.

Nevertheless, Zenith strode up to the Seeker's table and said, "Hello, Hugh. I've returned to GrahBhag on urgent business and need you to fly me to the Collectory as fast as you can."

Hugh dropped the playing cards he was holding and stepped back from the table. "At once, Master Zenith."

"Still your wings, Seeker." The low voice came from Hugh's tablemate—a red-headed woodpecker twice the size of her Earth cousins with triple their number of wings. "You're not leaving till you've settled your debt with the Rolling Thunder."

Hugh was obviously intimidated by the much smaller bird. The raven patted his feathers. "I seem to be a bit short. You'll accept my marker, right, Rip?"

"Not this time," said Rip. "You've owed me too much for too long. And you've lost more tonight. Pay up."

"Look, Rip, we're in a hurry." Zenith took Hugh by the wing and pulled. "We'll bring the Seeker right back, I promise."

Rip rose off the tabletop, her six wings beating fast as a hummingbird's. But instead of a hum, her wings rumbled like thunder, shaking the entire tavern. She bellowed, "None shall leave!" The lights flickered, then blinked out. When they came back on, the windows, doors, and fireplace had vanished.

Hugh fainted, sliding to the floor. Rip scoffed.

"Spare me the theatrics, Seeker." She waited for Hugh to right himself, but the bigger bird remained motionless. "Huh. Not faking this time." The woodpecker looked at the others. "One of you will have to pay or play in his stead."

Kevin pushed his friend forward. "Zenith will play."

"What? No I won't. What do I know about GrahBhagian games?"

The other customers gathered round the table as Rip dealt the cards. "The game is Dan Bun. Start with nine cards, discard three, exchange two with your opponent, then draw one. Whoever has the best hand of seven cards wins."

Zenith said, "This is ridiculous. How would I know what a good hand—"

The lights flickered rapidly. Rip rumbled, "Play the game or stay here. Forever!" Then she added more calmly, "Or at least until you've worked off what the Seeker owes me. If you win, the debt's forgiven and you can all leave immediately."

Zenith picked up his hand and went still. He dropped his gaze to the table, not knowing whether to laugh or cry at his unprecedented third lucky break. He knew this game.

The artwork on the cards was odd, but he recognized the characters. They belonged to a game called Abundant Bunnies, one of Apogee's old favorites. He was holding four black rabbits, two white bunnies, two brown bunnies, and one farmer. The black rabbits were the best card in the game, worth 3 points each, and he had most of them. The white and brown bunnies were worth 1 and 2 points, respectively. The only stinker in his hand was the farmer card, which was worth −3.

Now feeling confident and anxious to leave, Zenith tossed one white rabbit and the farmer to Rip, dropped three discards, and kept the four black rabbits.

Rip trilled, "Firman's in a hurry to lose." She dropped five cards and used her foot to slide two over to Zenith.

Zenith muttered, "I don't think so." Even if he got another farmer in return, he saw no way his hand could be worth less than Rip's.

Or so he thought. He'd been given one cleric and one guard, cards that didn't exist in Abundant Bunnies. The guard was worth 5 and the cleric worth 6.

If Rip had given him these, how valuable were the cards she'd kept?

The woodpecker plucked one card off the top of the deck, chuckling as she saw its face. She dropped her hand to the table. "A full hutch," she announced, and the spectators murmured appreciatively. She had one bun of each color, including a red rabbit, another card that didn't exist in the game Zenith thought he'd been playing. A guard, a cleric, and the farmer filled out the rest of Rip's hand.

Zenith placed his six cards on the table. Rip nodded her head. "Four black rabbits. A winning hand most of the time." She pointed at the deck with her beak. "You get a seventh card." Zenith turned the top card, revealing a frolicking rabbit with fur striped red, white, black, and brown. The card had no value printed, apparently worth nothing. Zenith dropped it in disgust.

The spectators gasped. One said, "He's drawn Dan Bun."

"The only card that could save him," said another.

A third laughed. "Gives him five of a kind and the win."

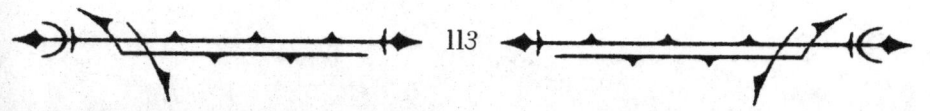

Rip rose off the tabletop, wings rumbling like thunder. The tavern shook, and the lights flickered as she bellowed, "Of all the rotten luck!" Then she settled, and the windows, doors, and fireplace were restored. She sighed. "You're free to go."

Hugh's eyes shot open as he lifted his head off the floor. "Well done, Master!"

The Scribe's Tent

THE SEEKER SANG Zenith's praises as they soared through the predawn sky from Threadbare to the Collectory. Zenith was pleased with how things had turned out at the Rolling Thunder, but worried that Apogee, the rebels, and maybe even the Wraith had beaten them to the Collectory.

His fears were unfounded. All was quiet as the Seeker landed in the upper branches of a tall tree. A solitary Royal Guard patrolled the rocky perimeter of the Collectory. Presumably the rest of the garrison was asleep in the nearby encampment.

Zenith said under his breath, "We need to get to Muncie."

Kevin whispered, "So, we sneak past the guard, is that it?"

Hugh said, "The guard cannot stop the Seeker

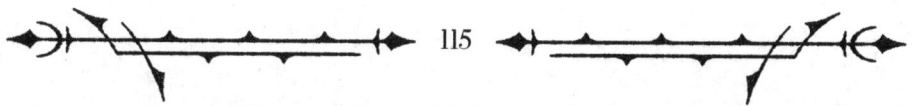

meeting with the Scribe. As long as you are all hidden, the guard won't intervene. The clerics are another matter. They've sequestered my poor brother inside a tent and watch him round the clock. Muncie's given little time to add the Details I relay to the Collectory, as the clerics insist he focus on restoring the Wraith to Its former glory."

Zenith and the cat exchanged a look. "Like I said, we need to get to Muncie. And stop him."

Hugh winked. "As luck would have it, the cleric on duty this morning is a bit lax. And there she is!" A husky brown-haired troll in a white robe crossed the rocky perimeter. "As I thought, Maggie's going for her morning tea. This is our chance."

Hugh lifted his wings. Zenith nestled under one, Kevin and the cat under the other. It was a bit rank, but it was also soft and warm. Zenith stayed motionless as the bird glided to the ground and hopped up the hill toward the guard. Nonetheless, the Seeker began to chuckle.

Zenith whispered harshly, "Kevin, Schrödinger, stay still. Hugh is very ticklish."

The kitten hissed back, "Schrödinger's *Cat*! And we *are* staying still."

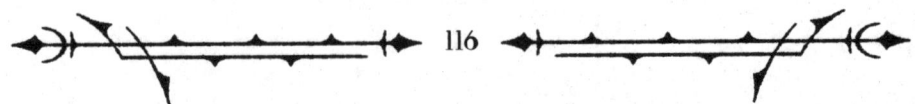

Hugh snickered, "There's no-ho-ho helping it. Just be quiet."

A moment later, a gruff voice said, "Good morning to you, Seeker of GrahBhag."

Hugh kept hopping. "And a good morning to you-hoo-hoo, worthy guard."

After a minute, the Seeker paused. Zenith heard the heavy cloth of a tent flap thrown back, and the Seeker hopped forward, chuckling lightly.

Zenith heard the Scribe say, "Amusing yourself with another one of your bawdy jokes, Hugh? No need to share."

"Actually, I ha-ha-have something serious to share, Muncie," said the Seeker. He lifted his wings as Zenith, Kevin, and Schrödinger's Cat emerged.

They were in a large, candlelit tent. Small green chalkboards and various colored pieces of chalk were piled on the Scribe's weathered rolltop desk. Nearby was a wire birdcage on a stand, inside of which Apogee's living physics book swayed on a swing. It seemed happy, and why not? Its need to be read was being fulfilled. The Scribe of GrahBhag looked decidedly unhappy as he intoned, "The Dread Outlaw Maelstrom."

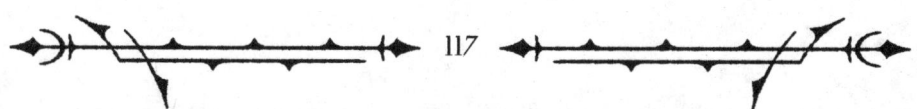

Hugh spread his enormous wings protectively. "Now, Muncie, remain calm."

Muncie did. The raven removed his gold-rimmed glasses and cleaned them with the tip of his wing. "Hugh, why do you associate yourself with this Firman trash?"

Kevin turned to Zenith. "I assume he's talking about you."

Zenith said, "I'm sorry to bedevil you again, Scribe, but you must stop what you're doing."

The Scribe gestured to the pastry atop his desk. "Eating my poppy seed biscuit?"

"What? No," said Zenith, thinking he wouldn't mind taking a bite himself. "I'm talking about your plan to transform the Wraith back into the Wurm."

Schrödinger's Cat padded forward. "And your reckless weaving of String Theory into the fabric of GrahBhag's reality."

The kitten cried and leapt back as Muncie lunged to peck her. "Be quiet, nitwit! I won't be lectured about my experiments by one of my experiments." The raven jerked his head toward Zenith. "The scheme you speak of is the clerics' plan, not mine. How dare they try to control the Scribe. To Gausia with the lot of them!"

Zenith scooped up the kitten and held her close. "So you're not helping them?"

"Just the opposite," Muncie whispered, glancing around. "I'm trying to destroy the Wraith, not return It to Its throne." He reached under his desk and jiggled something, causing a concealed drawer to pop open. The bird dipped his beak inside and removed a chalkboard, which he dropped onto the desk. "Took me a while to come up with something that would dispose of It without the clerics growing wise. They're always hovering, attempting to edit me. It's infuriating!"

Muncie took a deep breath and continued. "The final concept is ingenious, and yet the wording is deceptively simple." He knit his brows together as he stared at the slate. "But is it *too* simple? I'll only have one chance; I must get it right."

Zenith and the cat leaned in. The message on the chalkboard read, "The Wraith has been transformed into." The sentence was incomplete.

Schrödinger's Cat said, "Pardon me, honorable Scribe, but may I ask how you intend to alter the Wraith?"

Ignoring the cat, Muncie addressed Zenith. "Your wondrous science provided the solution. The concept's called a wormhole."

The cat sat up. "A wormhole?" She began to purr. "I see . . ."

Kevin asked, "Isn't that a sci-fi space hole you use to jump across the universe or travel through time?"

The cat shook her head. "Not a classic wormhole. A classic wormhole is inherently unstable and instantly collapses in on itself." She turned to the Scribe. "We are talking about a classic wormhole, correct?"

"Of course, imbecile." Addressing everyone, Muncie crowed, "Quite an elegant solution if I do say so myself. The Great and Holey Wurm becomes a wormhole, then immediately destroys Itself. And those clumsy clerics will be none the wiser until it's too late."

Kevin shrugged. "Sounds good to me."

"Yeah, it sounds great, actually," said Zenith. "What are we waiting for? Let's do it."

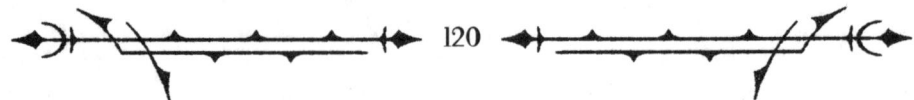

Muncie covered the special slate with his wing. "Well, as I said, I've got to make sure to get it exactly right."

Schrödinger's Cat nodded. "The Scribe's correct, Maelstrom. Science demands precision. One misplaced decimal point or one misspelled word . . ." The cat's hair stood up. "Hold on. Scribe, how are you—"

"We don't have time for exactly right," Zenith said. "My sister is coming right now. The Wraith is coming right now. We need a solution right now."

As if to underscore his point, a battle cry sounded from the direction of the Royal Guard's camp. Apogee's revolt had begun.

Revolting

THEY HEARD A voice shout, "Scribe! We're under attack! It's not safe here." The tent flaps parted, and in stepped the husky, brown-haired troll. The cleric's expression shifted from concern to outrage. "Traitors. The lot of you!"

Again, Hugh spread his wings to protect the others. "Now, Maggie, remain calm." With a savage yowl, the troll leapt onto Hugh's back and began pummeling him.

Muncie yelled, "Unhand my brother!" and pecked at the troll's head while Hugh bucked, trying to throw Maggie off. His flailing knocked out one of the tent's support poles.

Kevin and the cat ran past the combatants and out the tent's drooping entrance, but Zenith went in the opposite direction, toward the desk, scooping up the special slate designated to destroy the Wraith.

Sifting through the chalk pile, he found the Scribe's stub of iridescent enchanted chalk. He managed to duck under a loose section of the tent and exit just as it caved in completely with the troll and two birds inside.

The Collectory itself stood before Zenith. The last time he'd seen it, the mystical structure had looked sickly and withered. Now it appeared fully recovered, its green chalkboard leaves and rainbow-corded branches resplendent in the early morning light. Somewhere within its canopy was the slate he'd written that had inadvertently frozen his sister's age at four. The new slate he held in his hands would buy the time to find it, if the Scribe and Schrödinger's Cat were right about it eradicating the Wraith. They had better be. Because the rising heat in his scarred wrist told him the red phantom was rapidly approaching.

The mystical force of the Collectory was also acting upon his hands, pulling on the slate. *Not yet*, thought Zenith. *I need to see the fiend appear, complete the text, then watch It disappear forever.*

As if it had read his mind, the Wraith emerged from between two boulders on the crest of the hill. It stopped there and turned its awful, vacant gaze upon Zenith.

Aah Bah Cee, Aah Bah Cee. The chant burned deeper into his brain with each repetition. Fighting the rising pain in his wrist, Zenith used the enchanted chalk to complete the message, so the slate now read, "The Wraith has been transformed into the Wurmhole."

The new words glowed bright white. The fire in his wrist flared. He clutched his arm and gazed at the Wraith. Zenith thought he saw something shifting on its surface. He squinted and took a step toward the phantom.

From behind him, Schrödinger's Cat yelled, "Maelstrom! Wait!," startling Zenith and causing him to lose his grip on the slate. It flew to the Collectory, where an empty branchlet wrapped it in its threads. Again, the chalkboard glowed white, then faded. The Wraith's flames, in his head and hand, faded with it.

The cat batted at his boot. "Close my lid, I told you to wait! Tell me, how did you spell 'wormhole'? 'W-O' or 'W-U'?"

"'W-U.' Is that a problem?"

"It's a catastrophe. Science requires precision. 'Wormhole' is spelled 'W-O.' If the slate now reads 'Wurmhole,' then you've created something else.

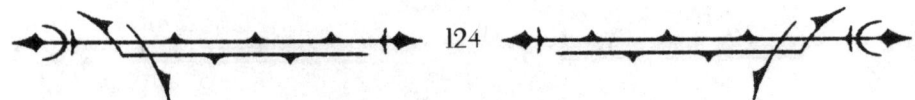

Something new and unknown. And possibly worse than before."

"Probably worse than before," Zenith said as he watched the black symbols that adorned the Wraith's crimson cloak slowly transform. Here was the bad luck he'd been expecting.

The Wurmhole

ONE BY ONE, the cryptic black symbols shifted into recognizable letters and numbers. "It's mathematics," said Schrödinger's Cat. "Equations that explain the theoretical existence of wormholes. But something is . . . off."

The symbols completed their transformation, then momentarily swelled forward from the red fabric before receding into the surface, sucking the surrounding cloth in after them. The Wraith's cowl contracted, and its cloak began to twist. Zenith was reminded of a wet washcloth being wrung out. He felt overwhelming relief. The Wraith was collapsing.

But it didn't collapse. It didn't disappear. It began to twirl, gaining speed quickly and shifting into the shape of a funnel, with its bottom flared five feet wide and its top tightened to a pinpoint.

The cat whispered, "Where's my box? I'd like to crawl inside."

Shouting and laughing, the rebel forces marched into view on the hillside opposite the Wurmhole. Leading the crowd was Old Timer, who spotted Zenith, raised his sword over his head, and yelled, "Yoong Maelstrom, the Final Battle for the Collectory is won! Three cheers for our leader, the Poison One, the Warrior Witch, Apogee Maelstrom!"

As the others roared, Apogee emerged from their ranks, flanked by Kreeble and Krobble. She was disheveled but appeared unharmed.

The Wurmhole would take care of that. The crowd's jubilant cheers died away as they spotted the transformed fiend racing toward them along the ridgeline. Zenith sprinted straight across the valley and up the hill. Apogee stood her ground, fists clenched. The gargoyles did likewise, even as those around them retreated. Zenith's feet slipped as he reached the steepest part of the slope, and he scrambled up the rest of the way on all fours, taking a protective position in front of his sister like a guard dog.

The Wurmhole stopped. It spun and hovered a few feet in front of Zenith, Apogee, Kreeble, and

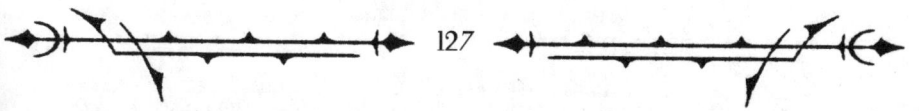

Krobble. The air around them crackled with static, causing Zenith's hair to stand on end. He didn't know what to do, but he had to do something. Whatever the Wurmhole was, it was his fault. Apogee couldn't pay the price for his rashness.

He bent his elbows and shifted his weight to the balls of his feet. He whispered, "Geegee, I'll attack and distract It. You and the others run as fast and far as you can."

Apogee choked back tears. "Zenith, no. Please! You're too smart to be so stupid."

Zenith smiled. "Oh, Geegee. We both know that's not true."

Without further warning, he leapt. But the Wurmhole was ready. As Zenith sailed through the air, the broad bottom of the twisting funnel tilted up to meet him. The cloak's hem formed a perfect circle, and the blackness within was deep and wide, whirling with concentric rings of white light. They were rushing at him, or he was falling through them. Whatever was happening to him, wherever he was going, it didn't really matter.

Because he'd tried to protect his sister and failed.

Elsewhere

SPINNING LIGHTS HURTLED past at breakneck speed as his body twirled and twisted. His limbs seemed to stretch. His head felt like it was being squeezed. He shut his eyes and vowed to keep them shut till his journey—or his existence—ended.

The cloak of the Wurmhole closed in around him as he whirled. Its softness surprised him. Its grasp didn't burn. The only pain was from what felt like a sharp-edged stone digging into his thigh.

His shoulder hit something that seemed like the ground but was unexpectedly crunchy. He bounced and rolled along inside the cloth till the cloak caught on something. Tumbling free, he abruptly stopped facedown, snow slapping his cheeks.

Panicked, Zenith pushed himself up on his elbows. He was in a snow-covered ravine with a few leafless trees. Between Zenith and the trees was a solitary bush half buried in a snowdrift. The snow was pristine, except for a deep, irregular hole, perhaps created by whatever jagged stone had been sucked inside the cloak with him. The cloak itself was caught on the bush's bare branches, flapping in the harsh winter wind.

Except it wasn't the cloak. The Wurmhole or Wraith or Wurm, whatever the fiend was now, had disappeared. This small piece of well-worn cloth was something else entirely. Its fabric was a soft mauve with deeper purple stitches depicting a set of children's building blocks. Each block was decorated with a letter or number in the repeated pattern of *A, B, C, 1, 2, 3.*

The wind carried two sounds—distant, intermittent cheering and the rhythmic crunch of snow. Some unseen creature was approaching, and whatever it was, however fearsome, Zenith didn't want it to see him first. He hid among the trees.

The figure that crested the hill appeared to be a little girl, maybe seven years old, her head lowered as the wind whipped her long hair, concealing her face. She wore bulky boots, thick snow pants, and a puffy jacket, all too big on her. Far from the menacing creature he'd anticipated, she was perfectly adorable.

Zenith ducked as she looked up and said, "There you are!" Her English was clear and accented the same as his, but he didn't trust his growing sense of familiarity. If she had spotted him, so be it, but he wasn't going to reveal himself. "Now, don't run away." She hustled forward and snatched the blanket from the branch. Grabbing two corners, she shook the damp snow from its surface, her tongue protruding with the effort. She wrapped the blanket around her head and body, creating a hood as she fastened a large safety pin beneath her chin. She tucked her hair into either side of the cowl she'd created, and Zenith got his first look at her face.

From over the hill came a crack and a splash, followed by loud, urgent voices. The girl loped toward the commotion. Zenith watched the retreating figure till she disappeared, his mind blank, like the snowbank before him. But buried beneath the blankness was one thought, one inevitable conclusion struggling to break through.

An approaching siren shattered his sense of isolation, and he followed the girl's footprints to the top of the slope. He shuddered from the cold and from the chilling recognition of where he was. This was Kalikov Park. Below him, a hundred yards away, was the frozen pond, a broken patch of ice near its center. A young couple and several kids were clustered around a pair of paramedics as they hoisted a boy onto a stretcher. A second stretcher with another boy was already being carried across the snow to an ambulance. The little girl who wore her blanket like a cloak trailed behind.

"That's Apogee," Zenith said aloud. "And the kid on the stretcher is me."

Elsewhen

AFTER THE AMBULANCE left and the crowd dispersed, Zenith plodded down the hill, out of Kalikov Park, and headed toward the hospital. He wrapped his long, GrahBhagian scarf around his face as he tried to wrap his mind around what had happened. The Wurmhole had transported him across space and time, delivering him back home more than a year and half *before* he'd left, on the day he and Kevin Churl had fallen through the ice on Kalikov Pond.

But this version of events was unlike either of the parallel sets of memories he had of that day. Now Apogee was neither a teen nor a toddler, but some age in between. He and Kevin had gone to the hospital before, but never on stretchers. Was this a trick played by the Wurmhole? Was he really here, or was he still trapped in the robe of the red phantom, his

mind distracted while his body suffered some hideous torment?

If this was all an illusion, it was a convincing one. The movie theater marquee promoted a holiday-themed film he remembered seeing shortly before the accident at the pond. And the local drugstore was still in the middle of a renovation that had been completed by the time he had first descended into the horrible bag.

As Zenith approached the hospital's entrance, he saw Kevin's parents hurrying from the parking lot. Zenith hung back, letting them get ahead, then closed the distance to eavesdrop on their conversation with the man at the front desk. Kevin was on the third floor. Presumably Zenith's past self would be there as well.

Zenith climbed the stairs slowly. Was there any reason to visit the third floor other than to satisfy his intense curiosity about this new alternate timeline? And how much could he learn? Was he going to interview this version of Apogee? His parents? Himself?

He reached the third floor and gazed through the glass in the stairwell door. A nurse talked briefly with the Churls, then walked away. Kevin's mom and dad

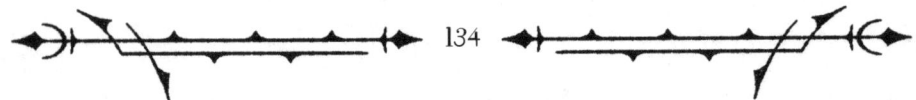

hugged, wiped their eyes, and stepped into the nearest room.

Zenith pulled his scarf tighter over his nose and mouth, then slipped quietly through the door into the hall. Medical staff rushed about, talking over one another. No one took any notice of him as he peered into the room the Churls had entered.

Kevin's parents huddled together by the side of his bed. Kevin was pale and unconscious, but an IV drip and several blankets seemed to be the only form of medical intervention. Did this mean Kevin was okay?

Zenith froze as Apogee shuffled out of the room three doors down, dragging her blanket behind her, then disappeared behind the nurses' station. He tiptoed down the corridor, peeking into the room she'd exited.

There were no bedside visitors. Like Kevin, younger Zenith was unconscious, but if Kevin had been pale, Zenith was ashen. A venous catheter was attached to his arm, his head was swathed in bandages, an oxygen mask covered his mouth, and his chest labored beneath a network of attached wires. Monitors beeped and pinged out of sync with one another.

Zenith entered the room and approached the bed, horrified and fascinated by his alternate self's condition. His trance was broken by the approaching voices of his sister and mother. It was too late to escape. He was trapped.

Bedside

ZENITH CLOSED THE opaque curtain dividing the hospital room and sat on the vacant bed. A moment later, his sister and mother entered, too caught up in their conversation to notice anything had changed.

Sounding weary, his mom said, "When I tell you to stay somewhere, you need to stay there. You're too young to be wandering around the hospital."

Apogee said, "I wanted to hear what the doctors were telling you."

"And I promised I would share what they said."

"I want the real story. Not the dumbed-down baby version."

"Honey, when you're an adult, sometimes you'll wish for the dumbed-down version." She sighed. "All right, Apogee, here it is. Zenith hit his head hard and

then he was underwater for some time. That could mean serious damage. They won't know for sure till he wakes up. He could wake up in an hour. Or a day or a week."

"Or never." Apogee's voice wavered.

"No one's saying that, Geegee." His mother didn't sound too steady. "We just have to wait and hope and watch over him."

"But I didn't watch him, Mom. That's why this happened."

"Oh, sweetheart, that's not what I meant. It's not your job to keep Zenith out of trouble. He's your *big* brother. He looks after you. He should've quit with the others when they saw the crack in the ice. Zenith's too smart to be so stupid."

"But if I'd stayed there—"

"What would you have done? How would you have changed things?"

Apogee had no answer.

"Geegee, I know you love your brother very much and you feel like you let him down, but what happened today wasn't your fault."

Zenith heard a third voice say, "Ms. Maelstrom?

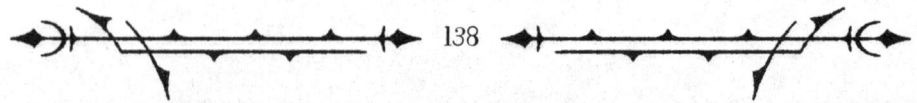

Can you come to the nurses' station? A few more forms to sign."

The sound of Mom kissing Apogee. "Stay here, Geegee. Talk to your brother. The doctor says it might help." A chair scraped across the floor and then there were only the machines, beeping mournfully.

Zenith sat still, worried the slightest noise might give him away. When he heard his sister softly say, "Zenith?," he stiffened before quickly realizing this version of Apogee was talking to the injured version of himself. "Zenith, I'm sorry." Her voice trembled more than before. "I shouldn't have rooted for you to play against Kevin. And I shouldn't have gone chasing after my blanket before you fell in. I should've kept you out of trouble. I should've made you get off the ice. I should've saved you." She sobbed softly.

Zenith wanted to comfort his sister and tell her everything would be all right. But if he revealed himself, she would be anything but comforted and everything would be far from all right.

"Oh, Geegee, come here." It was their father's voice. There was rustling and then Apogee's sobs became more muted. Zenith imagined her face pressed against their father's chest. "Mom's going to stay with Zenith tonight. I'm taking you home."

Apogee muttered, "I want to stay here."

"I know you do. But you've been out in the cold all afternoon. You need a hot meal and a warm bed. We'll come back early tomorrow. I promise."

Several minutes after they left, Zenith drew back the curtain and tiptoed past his alternate self. He made it to the stairs without being noticed, then climbed to the top floor and found an empty lounge. Exhausted, he flopped on the sofa.

He was flooded with love for Apogee. And regret. It hurt him to see his sister so solemn and sad. Her concern for him or, rather, his younger self, was matched by his own concern for her and her other self. What had happened to the Apogee back in GrahBhag after he'd inadvertently leapt into the Wurmhole? He'd committed yet another rash act and left her vulnerable to the very threat he'd been trying to protect her from.

The Wurmhole had taken him away from that Apogee and brought him to the day of the accident. Why? Had he simply been exiled to a time and place

that would cause him maximum suffering? Was this alternate version of himself doomed to die? Was he supposed to assume his other self's place?

He found no answers, but the questions continued to buzz in his head.

Intruder

A VOICE BUZZED IN his head. Zenith peeled his cheek off the vinyl couch cushion and opened his eyes. "I repeat," said the amplified voice from the loudspeaker. "Visiting hours are now over."

Must've fallen asleep, he thought. *Can't do that again.*

Silence. Then more buzzing. Zenith opened his eyes. The voice was saying, ". . . to the second-floor nurses' station."

Fell asleep again. Better get up.

He didn't. Sometime later, he stirred. The clock on the opposite wall was blurry, but both hands hovered somewhere between the four and the five.

That got him up. He wobbled through the hall and stumbled down the stairs till he came to the ground floor. He exited to the street.

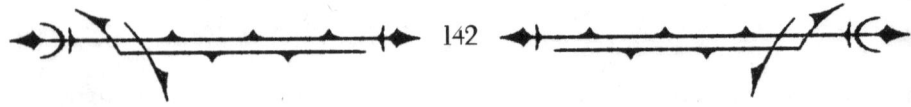

The bitter cold helped clear his head, though it didn't clear anything else up. He still had no clue why he was here or where he should go. He decided to head home, though he couldn't imagine being let in. *Hi, Dad. Sorry to wake you. No, I didn't recover. That's not me. I'm Alternate Timeline Zenith, and I'm from the future. Your Zenith is still in the hospital, and I thought since his bed isn't being used . . .*

It took a while to reach his house, the cold making his trek seem even longer. Skirting the pool of light cast by the porch lantern, he dashed up the driveway and over to the side of the house where the bedrooms were located. He peeked inside his parents' window, barely able to make out the lump that was his father on the right side of the bed. He moved past his own bedroom and stopped at Apogee's window. His sister's night-light illuminated the room, making it easy to see everything.

Everything but Apogee. She wasn't in her bedroom. But something else was. Zenith gasped, cold air stinging his throat. His hand went reflexively to the scar above his ear.

An old-fashioned doctor's satchel the size of a small suitcase slumped on the bedroom floor.

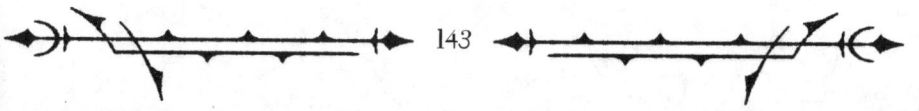

Apogee's night-light illuminated the bag's many mismatched pelts and the haphazard stitches holding them in place. The tarnished brass clasp, fashioned to resemble a rose vine, was open. Its numerous thorns turned upward like the fangs of a beast straining to be fed.

But the horrible bag had already been fed. Zenith was certain it had swallowed up his little sister. Perhaps a Shlurp had dragged her inside. Or maybe she'd entered voluntarily. It dawned on him that this was likely the trip during which Apogee had deliberately changed her age, becoming a teenager and altering events so that Zenith and Kevin escaped the frozen pond more quickly and in much better shape.

Zenith slumped against the stucco wall, stunned, ashamed of the uncharitable thoughts he'd harbored about his sister. Apogee hadn't insisted on being older out of some perverse need to boss Zenith around, but from a selfless desire to be his protector.

And now Zenith was driven by the same desire to safeguard Apogee. Perhaps the Wurmhole had sent him back through time to be lured into the bag when it was still the Great and Holey Wurm. Even if Apogee was fated to escape its clutches, the fiend might try to eliminate her interfering brother. But whether it was laying a trap or not, Zenith was going to find his sister and shield her from harm.

Moving to the backyard, he retrieved the extra house key from its hiding place in his dad's humble rock garden and unlocked the back door, by the kitchen. He slowly tiptoed to Apogee's bedroom. As he opened her door, it creaked loudly. From down the hall, he heard his father's snoring falter as his dad mumbled, "Apogee? You okay?" Zenith held his breath. But after a long moment, his father's snoring resumed.

Zenith entered, closing his sister's door gently. The plush carpet muffled his footsteps as he approached the bag and stared inside. Though its mouth was open, the link between worlds was closed.

Without hesitation, Zenith pressed his index finger against one of the clasp's thorns. He dangled the digit over the bag's gaping maw and fed it a drop of blood. The bag snapped shut and shivered with delight. Its surface shimmered in the room's artificial light; then the bag's mouth gaped wider than before. Cool air wafted up as if from a deep well. The vast, dark space seemed eager to welcome another visitor.

Or victim. The notion might've made him hesitate, but at this point Zenith felt, if not comfortable, at least familiar with the trials and tribulations of GrahBhag.

Zenith bent down close to the clasp and smiled at the thread tied there. *Clever as always, Apogee.* Zenith closed one hand around the thread, gripped the latch with the other, and lowered himself into the horrible bag.

Acquaintances, Old and New

ZENITH PAUSED AS the bag enlarged around him and the thread grew in his grasp. Then he slid down the rope quickly and landed with a thud on the bottom of the bag's cavernous interior.

He heard the jovial voice of Big Mouth say, "Well, it seems we have another visitor."

"Indeed," replied the sly voice of Little Mouth. "And I'm so full already."

As he approached, Zenith said, "If you're talking about my blood, sorry, but you've had all you're going to get."

"Oh, this one's quite rude," said Big Mouth.

"And ignorant," added Little. "And probably ugly. But then, all Firmankind are a bit hard on the eyes."

"You don't have eyes," said Zenith, but he

tightened the scarf over his face all the same. He went to the corner where Dry Mouth lived, but the youngest, friendliest mouth wasn't there. There was no third opening in the seam. "Wait. What's going on?" He backtracked to the first two. "Where's your little sister?"

Little Mouth scoffed. "*I'm* the little sister, nitwit."

"No, there was a third—Oh, wait—Maybe she doesn't exist yet."

Big Mouth clucked, "You *are* confused, aren't you? 'Doesn't exist yet.' Some sort of time traveler, are you?"

The foul mouths enjoyed a laugh together.

Zenith spoke over them. "Actually, I am."

The foul mouths stopped laughing, then began again, twice as loud.

"I'm not joking," said Zenith.

"Come now," scolded Big. "Your kind doesn't possess power over time."

"But our kind does," purred Little. "Tell me when you'd like to go, and I'll send you there for . . . five drops of blood."

"Three," countered Big Mouth. "I will take you on a tour of galactic history for three drops of blood."

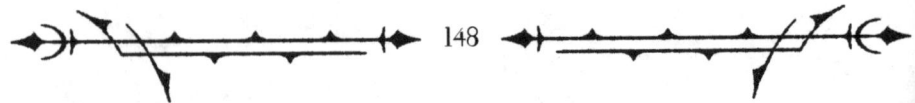

"You two are kidding," said Zenith. "Right?"

Explosive laughter followed.

"Forgive us," said Big Mouth. "But you are rather gullible."

"Not like the girl," said Little Mouth. "She was a shrewd one."

"That's my sister. How long since she was here?"

Little Mouth grinned. "You're the 'Master of Time.' You tell us."

"Oh, leave him be," said Big Mouth, feigning sympathy. "He's concerned for his kinfolk. We must endeavor to reunite them. For a price."

Zenith tried again. "How long since she crossed over to GrahBhag?"

Genuinely surprised, Little Mouth said, "You've heard of it?"

"Then you know," said Big Mouth, "that it is a land filled with wonder and merriment. A place where miracles are performed, fantasies are fulfilled, and destinies are altered."

"Spare me the sales pitch," said Zenith.

"No need for rudeness," said Big. "Your sister has crossed over to GrahBhag, and you wish to follow. Shall we discuss the terms?"

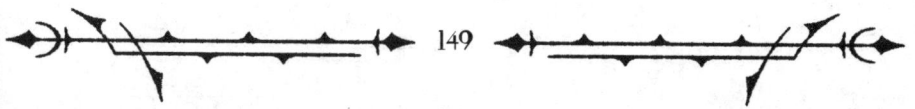

"You both know the blood that opened the bag was payment enough," said Zenith.

"Where did you learn that?" snapped Little Mouth.

"From that third sister you think I'm making up. Am I wrong?"

The foul mouths stayed shut.

"That's what I thought." Zenith looked between the two. "Now, open up and let me through."

Reluctantly, Big Mouth opened. Zenith approached, then paused. "And I expect you to be open when my sister and I return. Your other sister told me the blood we've already spilled pays for the passage home."

Little Mouth muttered, "I hate Future Sister already."

And then Zenith was tumbling through the dark tunnel to GrahBhag.

Treasure Trove

ZENITH WAITED IMPATIENTLY for his equilibrium to return after the topsy-turvy trip through the nothing-space connecting the foul mouths to GrahBhag. The air here was warmer than back home, but typically foul. The sky was the usual olive green of dusk.

He scanned the dense forest below him. Apogee might be down there, or anywhere else in GrahBhag. The trip through the Wurmhole had apparently neutralized his special insight. He hadn't the slightest inkling where she might be.

Time to strike another deal for the gargoyles' help. He spotted the small patch of open ground that held the hidden home of Kreeble, Krobble, Kribble, and Krone. Fixing the location in his mind, Zenith climbed down the hill and entered Whichway Woods.

Travel through the forest was never easy, but

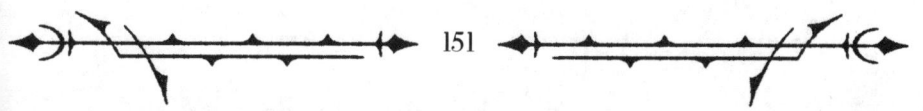

Zenith was used to the plants' treachery, and, with only a few wrong turns, found his way to the gargoyles' clearing. There were no creatures perched on the four columns that adorned the open space. Zenith assumed his friends had retired to their crypt for the evening and hastened to join them before the forest was blanketed in moonless night. As he'd seen Krobble do, he pushed the proper pillar forward on its hidden grooves.

One of the footpath's stones sank into the trembling ground, revealing the stairway that led to the gargoyles' underground sanctuary. Zenith stooped low and hurried down, then stopped abruptly at the bottom of the stairs.

There had always been a whiff of decay about the place, but now the rot was overwhelming. Zenith forced himself to breathe. Darkness swallowed him, but still he shuffled farther into the gloom, whispering, "Kreeble? Krone? Anyone home?"

A torch spontaneously combusted on the wall in front of him, casting its light across the sarcophagus, which had been a shattered ruin during his other visits, but was still intact at this earlier time. The lid of the burial chamber moved, stone slowly

scraping against stone as whatever was entombed inside sought to release itself. *Run,* his brain insisted, but his feet wouldn't cooperate. Fear and perverse fascination rooted his body in place.

The skeletal remains of a hooved animal's foreleg planted itself on the rim of the stone tomb. The other decomposed foreleg followed. Both legs shuddered with effort. A sickly rattle sounded as a pair of enormous antlers arose, followed by the skull of a massive moose. Bits of blackened flesh clung to the bones, which glowed a lurid blue. The ocular orbits were empty, but Zenith had no doubt this cadaverous creature saw him clearly.

A shrill voice sliced into his thoughts like a cleaver. *Kneel!*

Zenith's head throbbed. His hands flew to his ears as he doubled over. The pain from that single unspoken word was worse than anything he'd endured when the mind-invading Inquisitor had sentenced him to imprisonment in Eternity Tower.

Do not bend, trespasser, commanded the voice. *Kneel. Kneel before Draulic the Demanding. Kneel, kneel, kneel!*

Three sharp stabs at the base of his skull made

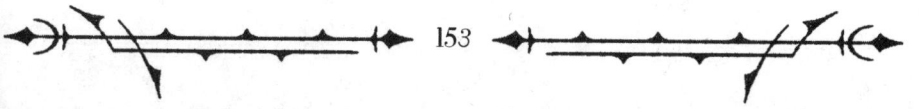

Zenith's legs buckle. He fell to his hands and knees on the stone floor.

The corpse climbed from its tomb, hoisting its massive rib cage up onto the edge of the sarcophagus before scuttling down the outside. *Get off your hands, thief. Show me if they hold any of my treasure.*

"Treasure?" was all Zenith managed to say as he sat back on his haunches.

Don't play dumb, bandit. Gaze at what you will never possess. More torches spontaneously lit, revealing a brass shield, silver sword, golden goblet, and a sizeable pile of precious jewels. The creature's hoard was scattered around its sarcophagus in an arc, like bait. Zenith also saw bones and viscera strewn about, presumably from past victims of this trap.

Though Draulic's spine was intact beneath its rib cage, the bones of its pelvis and hindquarters were absent. The revenant dragged itself across the floor by its two front legs, drawing nearer to the stupefied boy. *Choose your fate, scoundrel. Serve me or feed me.*

Zenith slurred, "What? Please—"

So be it. A blast of cold air hit Zenith as the fiend scrambled forward and leapt upon him, its hooves pounding at his chest. *Feed me, feed me, feed me!* Its

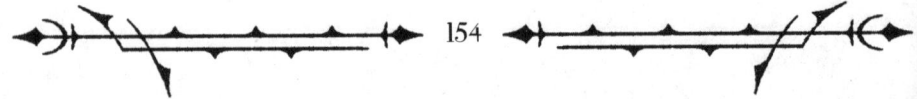

powerful jaws snapped at him, fangs grazing his throat. Zenith pushed against its cervical vertebrae and kicked at its rib cage, managing to squeeze out from underneath it. But Draulic kept coming, teeth gnashing as Zenith stumbled away. He banged his head on the earthen ceiling of the stairwell as he clambered up the steps and collapsed onto the ground beyond the crypt's entrance.

Come back, I command you! The skeletal remains of Draulic's leg rose from the crypt and reached for Zenith, but as the night air hit the bones, their surface began to bubble and hiss. The lower limb dissolved into an acrid blue smoke and the remaining stump recoiled as an agonizing shriek ravaged Zenith's brain. There was the clatter of retreating bones.

Zenith staggered to the column and, using his last ounce of strength, pushed the pillar back along its track. The stone from the footpath rose up again, sealing the chamber shut. His back leaning against the column, Zenith slid to the ground and passed out.

Pleasantries

DRAULIC'S TEETH PIERCED Zenith's throat. Blood gushed forth, red-orange in the torchlight.

He awoke screaming, his fists swinging at an absent foe.

The sky was light green. Something was chirping, though Zenith doubted he'd find any songbirds in the trees. It was morning in GrahBhag, and Draulic was in its tomb. More importantly, Zenith wasn't. But to say he was safe would be presuming too much.

He'd made a habit of presuming too much. He'd expected to find his favorite foul mouth upon entering the horrible bag, but Dry Mouth was yet to be. He'd assumed he'd find the gargoyles in the crypt, but they weren't there. The first mistake was harmless; the second proved nearly fatal.

He'd asked the foul mouths how long ago Apogee had entered GrahBhag, but hadn't thought to calculate how long ago it was in GrahBhag itself. Hours back home were equivalent to days here. So, if his trip through the Wurmhole had sent him back eighteen months in Earth time, it had to be decades earlier in GrahBhag. Would he find anyone he knew? Would anything be the same?

The idea of starting from scratch was depressing. So much so, his spirits actually lifted when, as he ventured forth, a tree root tripped him. *At least Whichway Woods still hates me.*

This relatively good mood lasted until he found Raggedy Albert's cabin at the edge of the forest. He could handle the forest's prankish malice. Albert's animosity was another matter entirely. Zenith gave the structure a wide berth, hoping to sneak by undetected, but the front door opened with Zenith in plain view.

"G'day to ye, yoong stranger." The speaker had the same squarish build as Old Timer, but he was gentler in demeanor and frailer of frame. He had a white bushy mustache and bifocal glasses. He picked up a rag doll, needle, and thread from the seat of a

rocking chair, then plopped down with a groan. His thick fingers worked on the unfinished doll with surprising dexterity.

"Good day." Zenith drifted back toward the cabin, attracted by the dollmaker's kindly manner. He cloaked his curiosity in a compliment. "You have a lovely home."

"Thank ye," the old man said without looking up from his work.

Zenith moved closer. "As you said, I'm a stranger here, and I'm wondering, can you tell me if there's a creature called the Scribe and, if so, where I might find him?"

Now the dollmaker did look up, his gaze quizzical. "Ye *are* a strange one. Of course there's a Scribe. Who else do ye think cares fer the Collectory and fer us all?" He returned to his work and hummed, "The Scribe's at the Collectory, the Seeker's in the sky, and GrahBhag is better for it, as ev'ry day goes by."

Zenith noticed what the dollmaker hadn't mentioned. So he said, "Praise be to the Great and Holey Wurm."

The old man paused again. "That one of yer Firman expressions?"

A grin spreading across his face, Zenith said, "Yes. Exactly."

The dollmaker also smiled. "Would ye like to have some tea and croompets before yer on yer way?"

His stomach grumbled loudly. "That would be—"

"Albert!" the old man shouted. "Hoory up with that tea. We've got coompany."

Zenith's smile faded. He began to back away. "Albert?"

The front door opened, and a living rag doll emerged, but this Albert wasn't eight feet tall. He was barely eight inches and overburdened by the silver tray and porcelain tea set he was carrying. His little mitten hands shook, and his high voice trembled. "I'm gonna drop it agin."

The dollmaker muttered, "Oh, fer Scribe's sake," and took the tray from Albert, setting it on the table beside his rocking chair. He looked at the unfinished doll in his lap. "I'll need to hoory up and complete this bigger Albert, or I'll never have a proper cuppa."

The little rag doll said, "Reuse me name if ye like. But don't try to reuse me soul for yer new Albert."

The dollmaker scoffed. "Plenty of souls ripe fer the pluckin'." Then remembering their visitor, he smiled broadly at Zenith as he poured the tea. "Cream and sugar?"

Zenith departed without a word.

Amusements

ZENITH HURRIED ALONG the dirt road with the stitched seam running down its middle. He grew wistful remembering how Kreeble had skipped back and forth over these same stitches on the way to his initial encounter with the Scribe. His first trip to GrahBhag seemed so long ago, and yet, in this timeline, it was still in the future.

Apparently, so was the reign of the Wurm. Zenith was cheered by the thought, though it was clear that many dangers still lurked in GrahBhag. He needed to find his sister, and with no better idea where to start, he decided to head to the Collectory.

The tree that wasn't a tree never failed to impress. Its chalkboard leaves shimmered in the red midday sun. Near its base stood the Scribe with his back to Zenith, facing his rolltop desk. Zenith walked counterclockwise above the valley, using the ridgeline's

large rocks to conceal his movement. As his perspective changed, he noticed Muncie playing a card game, then saw the bird's opponent was Apogee.

Zenith ducked behind the nearest rock. As far as Apogee knew, her brother was back on Earth in a hospital bed. She was dealing with enough strangeness right now and didn't need to think about alternate timelines. He planned to keep his distance as long as his sister seemed safe, and just then she appeared to be handling herself as well as always.

Apogee sat on the writing surface of the Scribe's desk in her baggy winterwear, eyes trained on her cards and tongue protruding from between her lips. Her beloved mauve blanket lay beside her. Muncie took a card from the draw pile, and Apogee did the same, her stubby legs swaying with excitement. She splayed her entire hand on the table. The Scribe threw up his wings in frustration at his apparent loss. Apogee made a grabby-hands gesture that Zenith recognized as "pay up."

The Scribe snatched a piece of aqua blue chalk from a pile and deposited it in Apogee's palm. She slid from the desk, ran to the Collectory, and ascended, disappearing into its branches, seeking a

blank slate. Muncie bounded after her, yelling, "No! Stop climbing this instant!"

Even unseen, Zenith knew the words she was about to write: "Apogee Maelstrom is bigger than her brother Zenith. She is a teenager! She's always been bigger. She's always kept him out of trouble."

The raven paced around the Collectory's base, muttering to himself, until a white flash from inside the canopy brought him to a stop. A lanky leg dangled below the lowest branch; a bare foot sought the ground. Then Apogee dropped into full view.

Apogee was over a foot taller than she'd been just minutes ago. Her comically short pants made it seem like all the growth had been in her legs, but the sleeves of her jacket were also short and tight. Her face was longer as well, though this change was more subtle.

There was nothing subtle about the Scribe's reaction. He flapped his wings and shouted. Zenith didn't catch every word of the bird's screed, but he heard "outrage" and "abomination" quite clearly.

Apogee seemed flustered. She handed Muncie his chalk and her now-too-small winter boots, then hurried away without glancing back. Zenith edged

around the rock he was hiding behind, keeping it between him and his sister as she approached. She climbed up toward the ridgeline and exited the valley a hundred feet from where he crouched. Zenith started after her.

"You there," shouted Muncie. "What are you doing prowling about? Present yourself to the Scribe."

Afraid his sister might hear, Zenith hurried down the slope. "Greetings, Scribe of the Collectory of GrahBhag. Uh, sorry for the skulking."

Muncie grimaced. "Another Firman?" He waved Zenith away. "Begone. I've had enough of your kind for one day. And take the belongings of the other. I have no use for Firman trash."

Zenith grabbed Apogee's boots and retrieved her blanket from the desk. He recognized the card game lying there. It was Apogee's copy of Abundant Bunnies. He reached for the deck.

"Leave the cards," Muncie snapped. "I want another chance to master this Firman amusement. Perhaps tonight I'll play Hugh."

Zenith nodded, bowed, and fled.

Retreat

ZENITH HURRIED BACK toward Whichway Woods. He assumed that Apogee, having aged herself up, was heading home. But because Muncie had delayed him, he'd lost sight of her, so there was no way to be sure. He'd come to GrahBhag to watch over her and had failed. Again.

His return route took him near the cabin. As he approached, the dollmaker came out onto the porch, hands behind his back. "Hello again, yoong stranger. Have ye any time for loonch?"

"Unfortunately, no," said Zenith, closer to the cabin than he preferred. "Have you seen my sister?"

The dollmaker put his thick finger to his broad chin and spoke louder than seemed necessary. "Another *Firman* like yerself, ye say? A sister, ye say?" He stamped his foot on the wooden porch.

A high-pitched war cry sounded from the shadows

below, and Mini Albert darted out, tackling Zenith at the ankles. The small rag doll packed a wallop, and Zenith went down on his back, hard. Mini Albert shouted, "I've got him! Recite the incantation!" as he tried to get his stubby arms around both of Zenith's ankles.

From behind his back, the dollmaker revealed his new creation. Medium Albert's body drooped between his hands, the blank button eyes facing Zenith. The old man intoned, "Iurp iohvk wr forwk. Iurp ulfkhv wr udjv. Iurp—Ow!"

A boot bonked the dollmaker right on his bulbous nose. Zenith lobbed Apogee's second boot, which hit his gut. Zenith shook off Mini Albert, sending the doll flying back toward the porch. Then Zenith stood, but before he could move, the rabid rag doll was charging at him again. Zenith threw Apogee's blanket on top of the doll and ran for the forest.

He kept running. And tripping and falling, but getting back up and sprinting till he was through the forest and up the hill. He stopped briefly before jumping into one of the two escape holes. He fell down the dark nowhere and then up into the chamber of the foul mouths.

"My, but we're busy," said Big Mouth. "This particular Firman family is a restless bunch."

Zenith sat on the floor, catching his breath. "So, my sister has already returned?"

"Some gangly lummox came through," said Little Mouth. "You insisted we stay open, so if some interloper has taken the place of your sister, the passage of the real one will cost extra."

Relief washed over Zenith. "No worries. That was her." He crossed the chamber, took hold of the rope, then paused. "Did you mention me to her?"

Little Mouth spat. "The less said about you, the better."

"Okay, good." Zenith began to climb. "I'd say I hope to never see you two again, but I know I will."

"More silly future talk from the Lord of Time," sneered Little.

"Oh, don't encourage him," grumbled Big.

Odd Man Out

ZENITH GRIPPED APOGEE'S rope, hanging below the massive clasp of the horrible bag. The exit was open, but everything was pitch-black. Day or night, some level of light should've been streaming in from above. Zenith slowly reached up. He imagined the giant brass latch slamming shut, crushing his hand.

His fingertips touched plastic. Gently he pushed against the foreign barrier. It popped up slightly, then fell back down. Zenith pushed harder, and it was gone. Dim light and cold air flowed in from above, as did the sound of distant traffic.

He let go of the rope and grasped the giant clasp. As he'd done at the end of his other trips, Zenith swung his body up and over the bag's threshold. Everything around him seemed to shrink and spin and topple. His shoulder hit a cold concrete curb, and he spilled onto a snow-covered street as garbage followed him out of the overturned trash can.

Zenith got to his knees and looked around. This seemed like his neighborhood, but it wasn't his street. Apogee had disposed of the horrible bag in some stranger's garbage can, blocks from home. He quickly righted the can, replaced its contents, and retrieved the horrible bag.

One darkened residential street looked much like the next, and exhausted Zenith headed in the wrong direction for some time before realizing his mistake. He corrected course incorrectly and became more disoriented. By the time he finally found his way home, the sun had risen and his family was having a special Sunday breakfast, visible through the large dining room window.

Zenith's envious stomach grumbled. Everyone was enjoying fresh-squeezed orange juice, bacon, eggs, and his favorite: Mom's homemade cinnamon rolls. He recalled this breakfast. It had occurred in the version of events with Apogee as the older sibling.

He'd fallen into the pond and received his seven stitches before being released to his parents. They'd scolded him for his reckless behavior, then expressed

remorse for reacting harshly in their fright. The following morning, *this* morning, they'd served him a fancy breakfast reserved for special occasions.

He supposed they had reason to celebrate. The incident on the pond could've turned out very differently. It *had* turned out very differently. But his sister Apogee had found a way to change events, possibly saving Zenith's life by making sure that she'd "always been bigger" and "always kept him out of trouble."

This wasn't some new alternate timeline. There weren't any alternate timelines. Just one timeline in which first Apogee and then Zenith messed around with her age and his memories. One timeline. One life. And the younger version of himself was living it. Where did that leave him?

After breakfast, his family settled in for a Maelstrom movie marathon that started with an action flick selected by his younger self. Zenith used the bombastic soundtrack as cover for a quick foray into the kitchen, where he snuck some leftovers and, feeling a little guilty, grabbed several fistfuls of quarters from the immense change jar.

Seeking warmth and a place to clear his head, he walked across town and slipped into the hospital as visiting hours began. Hiding his mother's cinnamon rolls under his scarf, he visited the cafeteria and purchased a small milk. The cashier cocked her eyebrow. "That it?"

Zenith nodded and retreated to a corner table that shielded him from her suspicious gaze. He furtively nibbled the cold pastry and puzzled over his predicament.

Whether by accident or sadistic design, the Wurmhole had stranded him in the past, where his younger self occupied his place. He had no role to play except as custodian of the horrible bag. As painful as it might be, perhaps the best way to protect his loved ones was to take the despicable thing as far away as possible and start a new life somewhere else.

But what would the consequences be if he prevented his and his sister's future GrahBhagian adventures from ever happening? If his younger self didn't eventually go through the Wurmhole, how would he end up here in the past? Might he, himself, cease to exist?

He considered another option. What if, instead of obstructing his future journeys inside the horrible bag, he intervened in them? He could track down

Apogee at the rebels' hideout in Canker Grove and tell her about the disastrous result of the attack on the Collectory. But if he did, would she abort her plans or accelerate them? By trying to make things better, either on GrahBhag or on Earth, he might accidentally make them worse. His milk seemed to sour as he realized that his mere presence in the past might've already altered future events.

He decided the safest plan was to let everything play out as it had before. Sixteen months from now, he would make sure the horrible bag appeared on his own front porch for younger Zenith to discover. He would shadow himself on his GrahBhagian excursions to make certain nothing had been altered, that no chaotic consequences of his time travel had sent him and his sister on another trajectory altogether. And, assuming his younger self entered the Wurmhole, he would rejoin the fight and prevent the Wurmhole from harming Apogee.

Because time functioned differently inside the horrible bag, those sixteen Earth months would be multiplied by twenty-four if he spent the duration in GrahBhag. So, unless he wanted to be a middle-aged man by the time the summer after next rolled around, he would have to mark time on Earth.

But how and where? Sneaking into his home and swiping leftovers had been risky. What would've happened if one of his parents, or worse yet, his younger self, had come into the kitchen? He could turn to the newly aged-up version of Apogee for help, but what could she do, hide him in her closet for months on end? And what if she'd already forgotten her journey into the bag? He imagined approaching his sister. *Hi, Apogee. I'm Time Travel Zenith. I'm from the future, where you're in danger from a creature called the Wurmhole. It lives in a bizarre world hidden inside a hideous bag. Wait, why are you running away screaming?*

An actual scream arose from the cafeteria's kitchen. A scrawny cook burst through the swinging doors and clung to the cashier. Prying him off and holding him at arm's length, she said, "Mickey, what the heck is wrong with you?"

The cook trembled. "There's something in there, Clara. Something unspeakable."

Clara groaned, "Oh no, not another *R-A-T.*" Without waiting for confirmation, she pushed open the double doors and entered the kitchen. A moment later, she speed-walked back out, grabbed Mickey by the arm, and led him out of the cafeteria, hastily flipping the sign from Open to Closed.

Apparently Zenith had been forgotten. He gobbled the rest of his roll, drained his milk, and headed for the kitchen. Lugging along the horrible bag, he was tempted to load it with prepackaged meals, but was ultimately repulsed by the idea of stealing and by the thought of consuming anything that had been stored inside the horrible bag.

He pushed the doors apart and peered into the kitchen. Something was in there, all right, eating noisily. The creature's head was jammed under the metal lid covering the grease trap in the kitchen floor. A spike-studded, scale-covered body wriggled as paw-like feet slipped on the slick tiles.

It was astonishing to see her on Earth. Zenith loudly cleared his throat, and Kreeble pulled her head out of the grease trap. Perhaps for the first time ever, she left a meal unfinished. She ran over, scrambled up the length of his body, and perched on his shoulder. Glaring at him, she said, "Where have you been?"

41

Visitor

ZENITH CLIMBED TO the lounge on the top floor where he'd slept the night of his younger self's hospitalization. Scaffolds and plastic sheeting indicated that the adjacent wing was closed for renovation. But no work was underway that Sunday morning. He took a seat and let go of the squirming bundle under his scarf. "It's safe now."

The gargoyle remained hidden. "I doubt that. Unless we have returned to GrahBhag."

Zenith tried to coax her to come out. "Why don't you tell me how you got here before we plan your departure."

Kreeble didn't budge. "I was attempting to save you from your own foolishness. When you leapt at the Wraith, I leapt at you, and I was lashed tightly to your side as the creature's cloak contracted. I instinctively turned to stone and was stuck that way for some time before I awoke at the bottom of a hole in a white-powder-covered field."

Zenith was moved by the gargoyle's loyalty, but simply said, "We call that substance snow."

"Call it what you like. The boot prints you left were distinctively GrahBhagian, so I followed them to this disturbing establishment, hoping you would still be here. With what I witnessed on my way, it is a wonder I did not turn to stone again and stay so forever."

Zenith nudged her. "C'mon. What're you talking about?"

"I am talking about your horrid world." She poked her head out, hissed, and ducked back under the cloth. "Why is everything so bright? Even at night, there are lights everywhere, each brighter than the largest bonfire. And those ridiculously fake white and yellow stitches that crisscross your terrain seem to confuse your kind as much as me, with everyone rushing back and forth. And the way you treat your transport beasts—ripping open their bodies and climbing into their bellies! How do they survive such abuse?"

Zenith rubbed his chin. "I'm not sure how to explain."

"Do not explain. Simply take me home."

"Yeah. It's best if nobody else sees you." Zenith sighed. Hadn't he just decided to stay on Earth? "But we can't leave immediately, and I can't stay in GrahBhag for long. Just keep hidden."

"Gladly." Kreeble burrowed deeper into the folds of his scarf.

Zenith slipped out of the hospital unseen and searched for a secure place to store the horrible bag, eventually settling on the bus depot. In the back of the station, there were lockers available for long-term rental, including tall lockers sized to accommodate garment bags or larger sets of luggage. After making sure he was unobserved, he wedged himself into one of these. He rigged the locking mechanism from the inside to keep anyone from stealing the bag, then nicked his finger on the thorny clasp and flicked two drops of blood into its mouth. Zenith dropped it to the floor, hugged Kreeble tighter to his chest, and climbed in.

Contraband

ZENITH PAUSED AT the bottom of the rope as his eyes adjusted to the dim chamber. Kreeble pulled her head out and sniffed. "Something about the air has changed. The Firman stench is gone."

Zenith scoffed. "Are you really ranking the smell of my home worse than yours?"

"The Lord of Time returns," announced Little Mouth. "Tell me, do all Time Lords wear such silly scarves over their ugly Firman faces?"

"Come now, sister," scolded Big Mouth. "No need to get off on the wrong foot."

Approaching the mouths, Zenith said, "You two certainly like to talk about body parts you don't have. Let's skip the useless haggling for more blood. I've already paid for myself and my companion."

Little Mouth snickered. "Firman babies are even uglier than the yetkinbroskas."

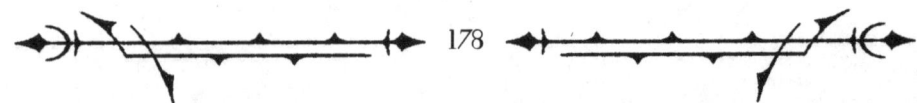

"Hang on, now," said Big Mouth, her jovial demeanor gone. "That's a GrahBhagian creature he's swaddling." She sounded angry and confused. "How did you smuggle it past us?"

"I didn't. It traveled back in time with me through a different portal."

"Balderdash," thundered Big.

"Ridiculous drivel," sneered Little.

"The pace of time varies between the Eleven Realms, but it never runs backward, young man," lectured Big Mouth.

"I must agree with these disembodied mouths in the floor," said Kreeble. "One can only travel forward through time."

Zenith was about to explain to Kreeble where they were in the timeline when Big Mouth's words sank in. Wide-eyed, he turned to Little Mouth. "You said my brain moved as slowly as time on Gausia."

Little Mouth laughed. "I said no such thing."

Zenith scratched the scar above his left ear. "No, you're right. Not yet. But you will. If I visited Gausia, would that mean time was moving slower or faster back on Terra Firmament?"

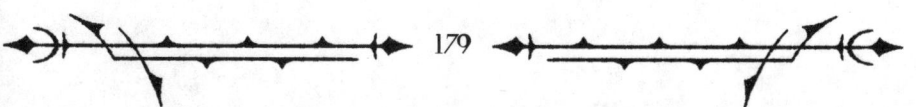

Little snickered. "How much blood is the answer worth to you?"

"Ignore my sister," said Big. "Neither of us has such knowledge. Nor shall we ever visit Gausia. And while *you* might, it would be a one-way trip. It's a toxic, volatile world fatal to your kind."

Big Mouth's words gave Zenith pause. It wasn't typical for her to volunteer information. To return the favor, and to compensate for the imagined smuggling of Kreeble, he offered each mouth one drop of blood, clutched Kreeble tightly, and passed through Big Mouth to GrahBhag.

After recovering from the discombobulating trip, Kreeble sighed with relief at the sight of the green sky, inhaled the foul air deeply, and scurried downhill. Zenith had planned to accompany Kreeble to the hilltop, then immediately return to Earth. Instead, preoccupied by his own thoughts, he followed the gargoyle. Perhaps Big Mouth had exaggerated the dangers of Gausia. If Zenith could figure out how to travel there, would visiting Gausia make time on Earth pass more quickly or slowly? With nowhere to live on Earth and nothing to do while he waited, could he refuse the chance to fast-forward through the sixteen months that needed to pass before he could follow his younger self into the horrible bag? He felt like he was missing another answer to his problem.

They were deep into Whichway Woods when it hit him. He stopped and exclaimed, "Grawlix!" Salty Mouth's home world. He hastened after the gargoyle. "Kreeble, wait! Do you know how rapidly time moves on a water world called Grawlix?"

The gargoyle sped up. "My visit to your world has ended my interest in foreign lands. Perhaps Krone can tell you something useful."

"Krone?" Zenith felt sick to his stomach. "No. Kreeble, stop. You don't understand. Krone isn't there." Panic distracted him, and a particularly nasty set of roots took advantage, ensnaring his left leg and knocking him to the ground. By the time he freed himself, Kreeble was long gone, undoubtedly headed to her catacomb home. But Zenith knew the crypt in the clearing didn't belong to her family yet.

It was occupied by Draulic the Demanding.

Crypt Keeper

WHEN ZENITH REACHED the clearing, the entrance to the crypt was open. He rushed toward the stairs, hoping he wasn't too late.

Kneel! The shrill voice of Draulic slashed through his mind. His legs buckled, and he tumbled to the ground, where the psychic assault continued. *Kneel, thief! Kneel before Draulic the Deman—Don't climb! I said kne—Get down from there!*

Kreeble's voice echoed up from the open chamber, shouting in what Zenith supposed was her native tongue. He crawled toward the stairwell before Draulic's piercing voice pinned him to the ground again. The pain in his head was offset by joy in his heart as he listened to Kreeble elude capture.

I said come down!

Kreeble yelled something fierce.

I'm not trespassing. You're trespassing!

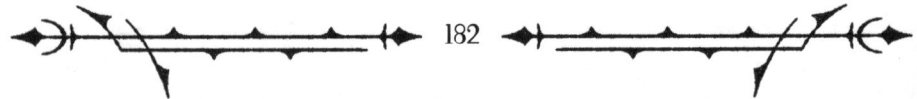

The gargoyle hissed and spat.

You impudent wretch. How dare you speak to Draulic that way! Zenith heard the rattle of bones and a pained yelp from Kreeble. A moment later the gargoyle scampered up the stairs. Zenith sat up and enfolded her in his arms, his fingers wetted by the wound in her side. The revenant's massive, blue-tinged skull and antlers appeared at the bottom of the steps.

Kreeble tugged Zenith's collar. "Do not sit there. Help me close the crypt!" She ran over to the column, pushing with no effect. Zenith staggered across the clearing as the voice tore through his mind.

Don't listen to that whelp. Obey Draulic. Come down here and bring the little thief with you.

Zenith summoned all his strength and leaned into the pillar beside the gargoyle. The pillar moved slowly along its track. But before the chamber was sealed shut, one last thought lodged in Zenith's brain like a dagger.

Dread the day that I break free!

Zenith fell to the ground, breathing heavily. Spots swam before his eyes. "Kreeble? Kreeble, where are you?" She'd escaped the chamber, hadn't she? He

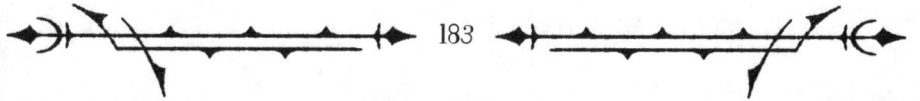

hadn't imagined it. That *was* her blood on his fingers, right?

"Rest a moment." Her voice was far away. Zenith closed his eyes. When he next opened them, the shadows were longer.

Kreeble sat before him, yellow leaves pressed to her wound. She said, "Do you think you can walk?"

"Let's try standing first." Zenith got up slowly, swaying. "Now, one foot in front of the other." He took a step and didn't topple. He gave the gargoyle a thumbs-up. "Cleared for takeoff."

Kreeble eyed him warily. "Do not take anything off. We may need your clothes for bartering in Bobbin." She took a few steps and waited for Zenith to follow. "Whatever there is to learn about these other worlds, we will find the information there. And on the way, you shall teach me about the diabolical sorcery of time travel."

Negotiations

Even in GrahBhag's most cosmopolitan city, a Firman was an oddity. Zenith and Kreeble had no trouble capturing attention, but acquiring information was another matter. The gargoyle grew cross upon discovering that Zenith was unwilling to barter away his valuable Firman blue jeans.

Absent exotic goods to trade, Kreeble promoted Zenith himself as a valuable commodity. As they moved from district to district, she acted as barker, attracting an audience for Zenith's street performance of "Firman culture": jumping jacks, a selection of North American birdcalls, and, for an encore, a recitation of the Pledge of Allegiance. Kreeble traded the silver they earned for food and lodging, but struggled to purchase any useful tips about Grawlix.

Their luck changed one morning while they

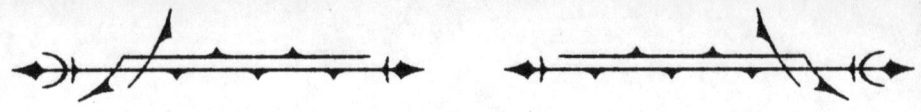

lingered in a musty antique shop, seeking shelter from a sudden rainstorm. The green-skinned shopkeeper approached them, her large reptilian eyes glimmering. "An honor to have a Firman visit my establishment."

Zenith had seen this acquisitive look before. "Sorry. My jeans aren't for sale."

The merchant chuckled. "Clothes are not my trade. But might I ask what you have in the compartments of those unattainable trousers?"

Patting his pockets, Zenith shrugged. "Nothing but jun—"

"Treasures!" Kreeble clamped her hand over his mouth. "Priceless Firman artifacts. My partner is unbelievably modest, which makes for bad bartering." The gargoyle flashed Zenith a look as she removed her hand and extended it to the merchant. "I am Kreeble."

The storekeeper shook it heartily. "I am Jafabel." She spread her arms to encompass the entirety of her cluttered store. "Tell me what catches your eye. I'm sure we can make a satisfactory deal."

Kreeble said, "We seek knowledge rather than merchandise," and began the elaborate preamble

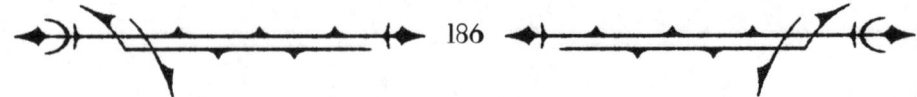

that preceded bargaining in Bobbin. Zenith's eyes wandered to a set of framed maps hanging on the nearest wall. There was one illustration in which the outline of North America was instantly recognizable, though it had been rendered crudely and was crammed together with Earth's six other continents. On the same piece of parchment was a second drawing of what Zenith assumed was GrahBhag.

Interrupting, Zenith asked, "What's this?"

Jafabel looked where he was pointing. "Ancient navigational chart. Helps the voyager locate the portals between worlds and calculate the time conversions."

Zenith and Kreeble exchanged an excited look. Zenith said, "Like how an hour on Earth takes twenty-four hours on GrahBhag."

"Twenty-five point five, actually." Jafabel sighed. "Less elegant, I know."

Zenith's heart skipped a beat as he spotted two additional images below Earth and GrahBhag. One was rendered in blue, the other bright red. "Grawlix and Gausia?"

Jafabel nodded. "The time differentials are noted. Though few ever visit such inhospitable realms."

Zenith crossed his fingers. "Can you tell me about time on Grawlix?"

"Certainly. While a minute drags by on Grawlix, a month passes on your world and around two years fly by on GrahBhag."

Zenith and Kreeble smiled at each other. The gargoyle turned to the shopkeeper. "I believe we have the basis for a fine barter." Kreeble nodded to Zenith. "Empty your pockets."

The results were worse than Zenith had feared. On the counter between them lay a chewed pencil stub, two gum wrappers, and a half-empty pack of tissues. He was about to apologize when he saw the covetous gleam in Jafabel's eyes.

Her forked tongue swept over her lips. "Treasures, indeed."

Grawlix

THE GREEN SKY was clear and the Scalding Sea glassy on the morning Zenith and Kreeble sailed for the portal to Grawlix. As luck would have it, Jafabel had more to trade than just maps and information. She also had a fisherman cousin named Flaajeb. In exchange for Zenith's precious Firman artifacts, Kreeble secured the use of his boat, his diving suit, and his services. Flaajeb was a surly lump of a creature whose sour mood might've been caused by the fact that payment had been made to Jafabel and not himself.

Gruff or not, Flaajeb delivered them to the designated spot swiftly and outfitted Zenith in the diving suit with practiced hands. Affixed to the inner wall of the round metal diving helmet was a large stopwatch, and on the other side of the faceplate was an inflated rubber air bladder. Flaajeb started

the watch and loosened the cork stopper on the bladder.

Ticking and hissing filled Zenith's ears as the fisherman secured his helmet. He could barely hear Flaajeb's reminder: "Got twelve minutes of air. Air bladder can't hold more. Four to reach the gate, one to spend in Grawlix, and seven to get back to the surface. I'll meet you back here in . . ." He consulted his pocket watch. "Two years."

Flaajeb nodded to Kreeble, who leapt into Zenith's arms and turned to stone. The fisherman pushed them both overboard. The boy plunged into the Scalding Sea and sank like the stone he was holding. As promised, the suit protected him from pressure changes and the extreme heat of the water. Although the air was stale, breathing was easy. Still, he couldn't help being a little jealous of Kreeble, who had no need to breathe while in her stone state.

He hit the ocean floor with time to spare. Or so he thought. The familiar sea vent was only a few yards in front of him, but the water, his suit, and the stone gargoyle all conspired to slow him down. Precious seconds ticked by with each leaden step. By the time he reached the vent, four minutes had

elapsed. Without hesitation, Zenith dropped into the gateway to yet another world.

He rode the same gravitational wave and undertow that had delivered him from the alley outside his therapist's office to the bottom of the Scalding Sea. He surged forward, then backward and forward again, losing hold of Kreeble, before being spat out of the portal.

He floated toward the center of an enormous treasure chest and settled down among gold coins the size of Frisbees, pearls as large as basketballs, and boulder-size diamonds. There were rings and necklaces scaled for giants. The smallest swag was a humble set of porcelain dinnerware.

"Octothorping GrahBhagians!" The voice came from a horizontal crevice between two wooden planks in the chest, a split that couldn't be accounted for by any aquatic disaster. It was a ragged rip in the fabric of reality. It was Salty Mouth. She spat up stone Kreeble and said, "Always dropping in when they're least wanted."

Zenith was surprised he could understand her underwater. He said, "How?," then clamped his mouth shut and checked the time. Ten seconds had already

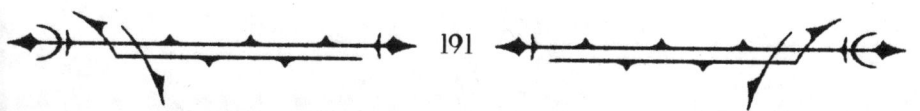

passed since his arrival. He waded slowly across the treasure chest toward the disagreeable portal. His air supply allowed for a one-minute stay, and it might take that long to traverse the breadth of the giant strongbox. He couldn't waste time, or air, talking.

Salty Mouth scoffed. "Another sparkling conversationalist from GrahBhag. You come here, grab a piece of gold, then leave with nary a word."

Unable to help himself, Zenith said, "Not GrahBhagian. Firman."

Salty laughed. "There's another bunch of asterisks."

"How would you know?"

"I've met your kind before. Had a Firman visitor just a week ago. Wasn't afraid to talk. And he was royalty—a Vy King."

Zenith laughed, then cursed himself for wasting the air. Thirty seconds to go.

"You calling me a liar? Huh? Speak up, you swirly-lined ampersand!"

Zenith let the insults roll on as he trudged forward, worried he'd already wasted too much time. With only five seconds to go, he scooped up Kreeble from where she lay and dove through the blathering

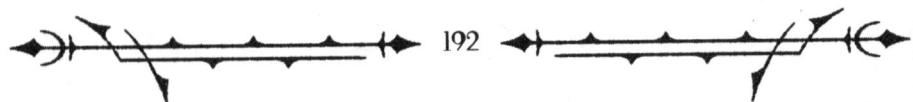

gateway. He surged forward and backward and then he was back on the bottom of the Scalding Sea.

As they'd prearranged, he patted Kreeble's stomach three times. She immediately shed her stone skin and swam upward, her hardy gargoyle physiology providing surprising lung capacity and protection from the deadly waters. Without Kreeble's weight as ballast, the buoyancy of Zenith's diving suit caused him to rise, although perhaps too slowly. Seven minutes were allotted for the return to the surface, and Zenith's eyes were riveted to the stopwatch as the seconds drained away. He heard the hissing of air lessen. The lime green surface seemed to grow no closer. And then, in the final seconds, it came rushing at him. He popped up like a cork, bobbing in the water, just yards from Flaajeb's boat. The fisherman checked his pocket watch. "Right on time."

Needful Things

"**Hurry, hurry,**" **murmured** Kreeble as she jerked on Zenith's scarf like a horse's reins. Zenith silently vowed to avoid doing the same with Hugh's scarf if he ever rode upon the giant raven again. But he understood the gargoyle's impatience. Ever since Flaajeb had confirmed that two years had passed on GrahBhag in the minute they'd spent on Grawlix, Zenith had been eager to return to Earth to check the time passage there.

But he'd promised Kreeble they would first check Whichway Woods for any signs of her family. Zenith wasn't sure the gargoyle understood just how far back in time the Wurmhole had sent them, but Kreeble insisted that Krone had lived in the catacomb for many years.

When they reached the clearing, Kreeble demanded they open the crypt, and despite his misgivings, Zenith agreed. The stomach-churning stench of decay wafted up. The torch at the bottom of the stairs lit spontaneously. Zenith said, "Nope," and pushed the column back along its tracks, sealing the chamber.

Kreeble slumped on the ground. Zenith nudged her gently with his toe. "Hey. Want to keep me company while I check on my home?"

She shook her head. "I would rather spend time with Draulic than revisit the terrors of Terra Firmament." She gave Zenith a faint smile. "Do not worry about me. I shall wait here on the off chance that this is the day Krone arrives in Whichway Woods."

Thinking of all he'd experienced, Zenith said, "Stranger things have happened." He left Kreeble to keep vigil.

After awkwardly extracting himself and the horrible bag from the cramped locker, Zenith ambled over to the bus station's departure board, trying to look like a traveler checking the time before leaving, which, in a sense, he was. His nonchalant act was undercut by his obvious delight when he saw the date on the display. A month *had* passed on Earth. He raided the station's garbage and recycling bins, placed his new "Firman artifacts" inside a plastic bag, took a long look around, then put the horrible bag and himself back in the locker.

In the thirty minutes he'd spent back home, most of the day had passed in GrahBhag. Kreeble sat exactly where he'd left her and refused to leave despite his cajoling. Zenith sat beside her as the last rays of the sun deserted them. Sometime later, he nodded off.

The morning air was cool on his face, but he felt cozy. When he opened his eyes, he understood why—he was wrapped in Apogee's old snuggle blanket. Its fabric was now dirty and worn, yet it was surprisingly warm. Zenith thought Kreeble must've tucked it around him, but when he sat up and called out, there was no response. At least, not from the gargoyle. The blanket responded by drawing tighter around him. Panicked and confused, Zenith thrashed about till the blanket released him. He scrambled to his feet and fled, pausing at the tree line to look back. The blanket was inching along the ground, coming for him. He ran through the woods and stumbled upon Kreeble gathering mushrooms for breakfast.

Zenith scooped up the gargoyle and kept moving. "You're going to have to take those to go."

Kreeble popped a mushroom into her mouth. "What has happened? Has Draulic escaped from the tomb?"

"No, it wasn't Draulic. It was something else. Something freaky. My sister's old blanket, it was alive and wrapped around me."

"Was it choking you? Smothering you?"

"Kind of. No, not really. It was just . . . I don't want to talk about it."

Kreeble tilted her head. "And yet you have begun a discussion of the very subject." She munched another mushroom.

Later, relaxing in the noonday sun, Zenith thought of the warm but unwelcome embrace of Apogee's blanket and regretted how he'd reacted. It occurred to him that, like the bat and the physics book he'd left behind during his first visit to GrahBhag, the blanket had an unfulfilled purpose. It was meant to provide comfort and warmth, and must've grown desperate to do so since his sister and then he had abandoned it.

After explaining his change of heart to the

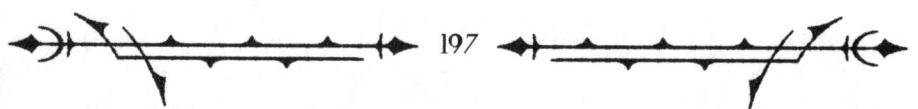

gargoyle, Zenith and Kreeble spent the afternoon searching for the blanket. As the sky turned olive green, Zenith suggested that if they spent another night in the woods, the blanket might come to him again.

On their way back to the clearing, they stumbled upon four sleeping trolls. Zenith shrank back at the sight of them, remembering the trolls who had presided over the Merging ceremony and his preposterous trial. But then Zenith noticed the smallest of them was using Apogee's blanket for bedding. He was relieved. Providing comfort to a troll instead of his adorable sister was quite a downgrade, but at least the blanket's needs were being met.

Working Man

AFTER SPENDING ANOTHER night in the clearing, Kreeble concluded that Krone was not likely to appear anytime soon. She was ready to jump forward in time once more. They left for Bobbin immediately, arriving at the antique shop near the start of the business day.

"There's no one I'd rather do business with," declared Jafabel as she ushered the pair inside. "Let's see what you've brought Jafa this time."

Zenith placed his "artifacts" on the counter, attempting to see them through the storekeeper's eyes. He guessed one of two items might garner the highest price: the empty potato chip bag or the crushed soda bottle. Instead, Jafabel raved about the plastic bag he'd used to carry everything. She wanted all his wares and anything else Zenith could lay his hands on. And in exchange for more Firman merchandise,

Jafabel and Flaajeb would facilitate as many trips to Grawlix as needed to return Zenith and Kreeble to their proper place in time.

"Excellent," said Kreeble.

"How soon can we leave?" asked Zenith.

Jafabel's broad smile faded. "Well, that's one thing that's nonnegotiable. Flaajeb absolutely refuses to take you there more than once a month."

"Unacceptable!" snapped Kreeble.

"Why?" asked Zenith.

"In sea-diving parlance, it's called the twists. Dive too frequently, surface too rapidly, or run too low on air, and you will suffer dreadful, possibly deadly agonies."

Zenith sighed. "Yeah, we've got something similar on my world. But this sounds worse."

The smile returned to Jafa's face. "If I may suggest an addendum to our deal, in exchange for food, shelter, and a modest amount of silver, the two of you could work for me between visits to Grawlix."

Zenith and Kreeble exchanged glances, then nodded in unison. A celebratory midmorning meal was shared and then they were put to work.

Zenith's duties included dusting, polishing, and

endlessly rearranging the merchandise. This left Jafabel free to attend to customers and tinker in her workshop, fixing old music boxes and broken clocks. Meanwhile, shrewd Kreeble scoured the back alleys of Bobbin in search of items that could be acquired at competitive prices.

During the daily siesta, Zenith often imagined swapping jobs. He knew he couldn't match Kreeble's negotiating and linguistic skills, but much to his surprise, he found he missed the monstrous multitudes that had once crowded in close for his street performances. Delight looked the same on any face, no matter the number of eyes. And, truth be told, he no longer found GrahBhagian faces that strange or frightening.

Finally, word came that Flaajeb was ready to return them to Grawlix. The second trip went smoothly, although Salty Mouth's mood remained foul. Given how little time had passed on Grawlix, her last conversation with Zenith was still fresh in her mind, and she was eager to resume their spat. Zenith was amazed by how many insults she could pack into a single minute.

And he was amazed by how much dust could

gather on Jafa's untended merchandise in two years. Upon returning, Zenith said, "I don't remember taking all the cleaning rags with me."

Jafabel slapped his arm playfully. "You know I get preoccupied with my projects." She made it up to him with a celebratory dinner. Kreeble watched politely, then dined on Zenith's ear grits before bed.

The next morning Jafabel allowed Zenith to sleep late. By the time he emerged from his room, the shop was already open. Jafa was near the front door, conversing with the four trolls Zenith had seen camping in Whichway Woods two years earlier. The shortest one now had Apogee's old blanket tethered on a chain with a constrictive metal collar. She leaned toward Jafabel, saying, "But if we *could* get our hands on it, could you sell it?"

"Of course!" Jafabel scoffed. "It's worth a king's ransom. It *is* a king's ransom. But many have tried what you're proposing, Corgia. All have failed."

Corgia yanked the blanket's chain. "I tell ya, Jafabel, this thing is strong enough to wrestle a multunus."

"Blue Bones guards its treasure with a ferocity unmatched by any beast."

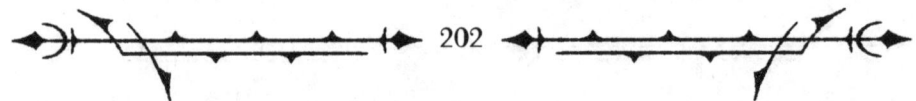

The troll spotted Zenith. "I'll prove my pet is up to the task." She unlocked the blanket's collar and whistled to it. Before Zenith could react, the blanket wriggled across the floor and wrapped itself around him, pinning his arms to his side. Zenith stood helpless, unable to break the blanket's grasp.

Corgia said, "See? With the proper planning, Blue Bones will be just as powerless."

Furious, Jafabel said, "Get that thing off him!"

"I was just trying to—"

"Get it off him and get out of my shop!"

"All right, all right." The other trolls retreated while Corgia whistled for her pet. Still the blanket clung to Zenith. The troll yelled, "Oi! Come here! *Now!*" Reluctantly, the blanket released Zenith and undulated across the floor to its master, who kicked it, chained it up again, and hissed, "You miserable worm."

The Rise of the Wurm

JAFABEL RAN HER webbed fingers along Zenith's arms, looking for injuries. "Please forgive me, dear boy. I should've never let such trash into my shop. Take the day off by way of apology."

"It's all right, Jafa." He covered her webbed hand with his and squeezed. "I'd rather work if it's all the same to you." Zenith polished the nearest curio until Jafabel reluctantly withdrew. He moved absentmindedly down the aisle, swiping at items with his dustcloth while ruminating on what he'd witnessed. The troll's cruel nickname for Apogee's abused blanket had to be a coincidence. How could such a pitiful, albeit strong, creature become the Great and Holey Wurm?

But supposing that was the blanket's destiny, could Zenith do anything to stop it? He felt a pang for the creatures of GrahBhag, knowing the suffering the Wurm would inflict on them. But as tempting as it might be to try to prevent its rise, he couldn't waver in his commitment to nonintervention. His mere presence in the past, not to mention his living in GrahBhag and traveling to Grawlix, might've already created unintended consequences. He couldn't take any further risks with his family's future.

Zenith turned his attention to the practical task of getting the shop back in shape. But after a few days, Jafabel insisted he take time to visit home and see what Firman artifacts he could find.

Back in his hometown, he took a brief walk to enjoy the spring weather while collecting wares for Jafa from various trash cans. Then it was back to the bus station and through the bag to GrahBhag. He needed to check on Kreeble, who'd gone to see if this second time jump had brought her family to Whichway Woods. Zenith approached the clearing, hoping for Kreeble's sake that the gargoyles were now in residence.

Stop right there! The shrill voice of Draulic the Demanding cut into Zenith's brain, dropping him to his knees. *Go more slowly and handle my treasure with care.* Confused, Zenith fought through disabling pain and raised his bowed head.

Two of the trolls from Corgia's gang carried a tarp with Draulic's sword, shield, goblet, and jewels piled on top. They made slow progress from the crypt's entrance to a wooden cart. Corgia herself was hitched up to the wagon and constrained by the tight metal collar around her neck.

Gripping the attached chain was Draulic the Demanding. Its skeletal remains slouched in the driver's seat, swathed in Apogee's blanket, the shape of its prominent bones visible through the tightly stretched cloth. It had shed its massive antlers, but its elongated skull and large rib cage were tucked close together, its cervical vertebrae compressed between.

Watch it, you oafs! scolded Draulic as the trolls' grip on the tarp slackened and a ruby rolled off the edge. The last lumbar vertebra of Draulic's blue-tinged spine inadvertently poked out from under the protective blanket. The creature's psychic scream immobilized Zenith and the trolls as blue smoke wafted from under the blanket's edge.

Cowering on the ground, Zenith guessed what must've happened. The trolls had tried to use the

blanket's iron grip to restrain "Blue Bones" while they raided its treasure. Instead, the blanket had liberated the living corpse from its burial chamber, protecting Draulic from the open air that would've otherwise vaporized it. Draulic had apparently celebrated its freedom by enslaving three of the trolls and had probably fed on the missing fourth.

Perhaps now it will feed on me. The thought should've gotten him moving, but Zenith was in too much pain. Luckily, Kreeble was hiding nearby, and she managed to drag him to his feet. The farther they got from the clearing, the better Zenith felt, until eventually he was sprinting across the open ground between the woods and the cliffs above Bobbin. After that, Zenith and Kreeble avoided Whichway Woods for the rest of the month.

Another trip to Grawlix, another outburst from Salty Mouth, and another two years passed on GrahBhag. Jafabel welcomed them back warmly again, but then did her best to appear stern as she said, "After this evening's celebration, I must insist that Zenith travel to Terra Firmament straightaway, as our supply of artifacts is completely exhausted and the demand for them great."

He left early the next morning, promising Kreeble he would check in at the clearing. Zenith crossed his fingers that Draulic was now far from Whichway Woods. Hopefully some brave creature had ripped the shroud from the obscene ghoul's skeleton, vaporizing its bones and banishing its corrupt soul.

No such luck.

Passing by the dollmaker's cabin, Zenith was stricken by one of Draulic's telepathic tirades. The pain was great, but Zenith's curiosity was greater. Sensing that something momentous was happening, he lumbered toward the cabin and peered through its window.

Two trolls held the dollmaker's arms while Corgia restrained Medium Albert. The tip of Draulic's silver sword pressed against the stitches attaching the living rag doll's head to his body. The hilt was concealed beneath Apogee's blanket, where Draulic dwelled, though it looked like the bulk of its remains had greatly diminished. The elements must've been eating away at Draulic a bit at a time.

Zenith winced as the voice sizzled in his head again. *Do as I command, spell-weaver. Use your magic to merge my soul with the fabric of my garment.*

The dollmaker protested. "But 'tis already a spirit inhabitin' the cloth. No tellin' what'll happen with two entities sharin' a single corporeal form."

Draulic pressed the tip of its sword into Medium Albert's neck. *Commence the ceremony!* Medium Albert gazed at his creator imploringly.

The incantation was indecipherable, but the results were terrifyingly familiar. As the dollmaker intoned, a violent wind whipped through the woods and into the cabin. It swirled around the room and rushed under the blanket. Zenith hoped for another psychic scream. While painful to endure, it might signal the failure of the ceremony and the end of Draulic's unnatural existence. But all was silent as the bulk inside the blanket vanished and a voluminous cloud of blue smoke billowed out from beneath its edge.

The pain Zenith had anticipated flared up, but not in his head. Instead, the A-shaped scar on his wrist burned as the blue cloud condensed, then was sucked into the surface of the cloth, which shifted in color from soft mauve to strident purple. New threads materialized along the blanket's ragged borders, weaving themselves into its fabric as it grew in size. The blanket levitated as its two long sides folded themselves inward, like arms savoring an embrace. These lengthwise edges met, then swiftly sewed themselves together, stopping short of the top. The resulting opening transformed into a cowl. And as Zenith looked on, the purple stitching on what had once been his sister's beloved blanket darkened to black, the numbers and letters morphing into the cryptic symbols of the Great and Holey Wurm.

A chant arose unbidden inside Zenith's head. *Aah Bah Cee, Aah Bah Cee, Aah Bah Cee.*

It continued uninterrupted as another, shriller voice responded impatiently, *All right, all right! We know what we want. We know who we want.* The newly formed figure of the Wurm floated toward the dollmaker. *Well done, servant. But we have further need of your magic. We must be joined with another entity.*

The dollmaker shook his head violently. "No! No, I won't do it." The trolls tightened their grip on the dollmaker's arms as the Wurm's cowl drifted toward his face.

We are not asking. We are telling. We will find the knowledge we seek.

The Wurm pressed the top of its hood into the dollmaker's forehead as the old man writhed and screamed. The acrid aroma of the dollmaker's searing flesh drove Zenith away. He stumbled through the woods and up the hill in a daze.

49

First Child

BACK ON EARTH, shock gave way to panic. Zenith had no doubt about with whom the Wurm wished to join. The blanket's spirit yearned for "Aahbahcee," who had loved it intensely for so many years. It needed to embrace and enfold Apogee the same way Zenith's bat needed to be swung or Apogee's physics book needed to be read.

Zenith tried to tell himself the Wurm wouldn't find his sister until next summer. But it seemed that his presence in the past had fostered the creation of the Wurm. Maybe it had also accelerated events.

Of one thing he was certain—something would still have to exit the bag if the Wurm wanted to snatch his sister. So Zenith held the bag tight, keeping the clasp closed and trying to ignore its sickening, pulsating warmth.

For hours he wandered, ducking into a coffee

shop, the hospital lobby, the library, anywhere he thought he might blend in. But a haggard boy with bizarre baggage drew attention, so he never stayed in one place for long.

Eventually he made his way to Kalikov Park, which, despite the warm weather, was sparsely populated on a weekday. He sat down on an isolated bench and gazed at the pond. His mind was flooded by contradictory memories—fourteen-year-old Apogee sliding toward him and Kevin as they flailed in the icy water; four-year-old Apogee blowing her shrill whistle until help arrived; seven-year-old Apogee trudging toward the ambulance, and later, venturing to GrahBhag. But in all these conflicting versions of that day there was one constant—Apogee had acted bravely to save Zenith from the consequences of his actions, and she'd suffered as a result. It was his rashness that had propelled his sister into the horrible bag.

Zenith racked his brain trying to find a way to keep Apogee safe. He thought of tying a heavy chain around the horrible bag and tossing it in the pond. Then he pictured a multunus rising up and dragging his sister underwater. It seemed ridiculous, but who knew what forces the Wurm might harness as it rose to power? His head swam with nightmare scenarios and then actual nightmares as, despite himself, Zenith fell asleep.

Sometime later, he was awakened by a girl's scream. It was dark out. His hands were empty. The horrible bag sprawled on the bench beside him, its mouth gaping. The scream echoed from the bag's depths.

"No, no, no!" Zenith grabbed the bag and stood, frantic. He spotted a nearby thicket of shrubs and plunged into it, thorns piercing his flesh as he sought the densest cluster in which to hide the horrible bag. Wedging it against a woody stem in the center, he shook his bloodied hand into the bag's open maw and climbed inside.

He wasted precious minutes trying to pry information from the foul mouths. Finally, for two extra drops of blood, they revealed a girl had been taken, and for another two, added that they'd overheard that the captor's destination was Stoating.

Zenith hurtled across GrahBhag, traversing mountainous terrain. His fears were seemingly confirmed. Apogee was to be sacrificed in an earlier Merging ceremony. And this time Zenith had no chalkboard, no magic chalk, no way to stop it.

By the time he arrived in Stoating, the ritual was already underway. Unlike the Merging ceremony he'd once interrupted, trolls made up most of the audience and no cleric presided. The Wurm hovered amid the circle of nine black lava rock pillars as the screaming wind swirled into its expanding hood. Glowing symbols on its cloak and identical symbols etched into the exposed face of the ninth pillar flashed sporadically. A girl floated slowly toward the living vortex, her hair and clothes fluttering furiously around her.

Zenith staggered forward, burdened now by the blazing agony in his wrist and the voice in his head chanting, *Aah Bah Cee, Aah Bah Cee.* He was too slow. He was too late. He was not going to save his sister. But he did not give up, and neither did the girl. In one last act of defiance, she turned away from the awaiting abyss.

She wasn't Apogee. Joy swept through him, then dissipated. She wasn't Apogee, but he recognized this girl. Carol Briar locked eyes with Zenith for a moment, and then she was gone, her body engulfed by the Wurm as the whole world glowed white.

The blinding light faded away. The wind ceased howling and the attendees stood quiet and stoic. There was silence in Stoating.

But the chant inside Zenith's head became a scream of agony and confusion. The shrill voice shrieked, *No? Not who we want?* Anger flared, then subsided, replaced by eagerness. *Then . . . we can feed.*

The body of the Wurm contorted. There was a loud snap and a grisly crunching as something moist permeated the cloak from the inside, altering its color from purple to red. *I'm watching It eat Carol,* Zenith thought, and bit his lip to hold back a scream. He saw new threads materialize at the hem of the cloak, lengthening and expanding it. Finally, the obscene feast ended. Again, merciful silence.

The stillness was broken by retching, as a bulge grew within the Wurm and rose up to its cowl. A black mass was disgorged. Nine spindly legs rose up from inside the coughed-up hairball and lifted a goo-covered body off the ground. As the firstborn Shlurp began to skitter away, the hem of the Wurm snaked out, grabbing its child and yanking it back under its cloak.

The Wurm's first voice wept and whimpered.

The second shrill voice responded impatiently, *All right! We'll keep this one while we search for the One.* The first voice began to chant again, sounding more insistent than before.

Aah Bah Cee. Aah Bah Cee. Aah Bah Cee.

Befuddled

STOMACH AND MIND in turmoil, Zenith fled Stoating. He relived the sickening consumption and transformation of Carol Briar, who'd attended his school, whose disappearance had been the first of many in the tri-state area.

He pictured the Wurm at the failed ceremony with Apogee, many GrahBhagian years in the future. How many children of the Wurm lurked under its cloak by then? How many girls would be sacrificed to the fiend as it searched for his sister?

He returned to the antique shop, relieved to see Kreeble and Jafabel. They were happy to see him, but alarmed by his state. Jafa insisted he sit down, then made him his favorite tea. As he sipped it, Zenith told them all that had happened.

When he'd finished, he looked toward the door. "Maybe I should go back to Earth and lock up the

bag. Try to stop the Wurm from merging with all those poor girls."

Kreeble shook her head. "Why do you think the results will be any different? Time travel is a befuddling magic. In both lines of time, the original and the one where you held the bag, the Wurm got Its clutches on this girl. Some events are clearly unalterable."

Zenith sighed. "Maybe you're right. But if I can't save all the girls, then I want to get to the one girl I *can* save. I want to get to Apogee." He kicked the coffee table. "Now!"

Jafabel swatted his shoulder. "Careful with the merchandise."

"Sorry. It's just so frustrating; I need to jump forward more than an Earth year, and each trip to Grawlix only moves us up a month."

Waving her webbed hands, Jafabel cried, "Hold on, I have just the thing!" She went to her workshop, then returned. "Been keeping it secret till I was sure it would work." She carried something lumpy covered with stitches, patches, and glue.

Zenith said, "That's the ugliest pillow I've ever seen."

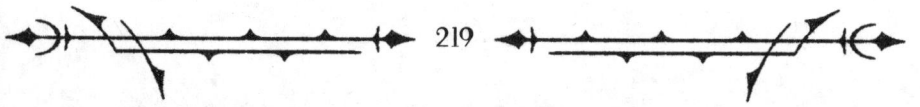

Jafa rolled her eyes. "It's an air bladder, silly. I've joined two regular ones together. Doubles the supply of air. You'll be able to stay in Grawlix much longer and leap forward to the point in time you seek."

Double Trouble

FLAAJEB SAID, "YOU have twenty-four minutes of air. Four to reach the gate, *thirteen* to spend in Grawlix, and seven to get back to the surface." The fisherman did his best to position the bulky double air bladder away from Zenith's face, then loosened its cork stopper and secured the diving helmet. "I'll meet you back here in . . ." He consulted his pocket watch. "Twenty-six years." He thrust stone Kreeble into Zenith's arms and shoved the boy overboard.

Zenith watched the seconds tick by as he sank. Jafabel had assured him she'd tested the air capacity of this larger bladder several times. Based on the date of his last visit to Earth, she'd used the ancient navigational chart to make more precise calculations and had assured him that thirteen minutes in Grawlix would give him a buffer of three Earth days before

his younger self's first GrahBhagian adventure was to begin. Zenith needed to make sure he returned in time to retrieve the horrible bag from its hiding place in Kalikov Park and deliver it to the front porch when younger Zenith was slated to discover it.

He hit the ocean floor and entered the portal right on schedule. With practice, he'd grown more skillful at riding the gravitational wave, and he floated out gracefully into the center of the enormous treasure chest, holding stone Kreeble securely against his suit.

Salty Mouth was not impressed. "Well, look at the bilge rat that's washed up on my shore."

Zenith turned to face her. "How can you have an underwater shore?"

"I'm using language metaphorically. Skull and crossbones, you're as thick as an anchor."

Zenith started moving leisurely toward the living portal. Still twelve minutes to go. "Give me every insult you've got. Today I've got time to spare."

Salty Mouth scoffed. "And who says I want you sticking around? Stop your lollygagging and be on your way."

When Zenith didn't speed up, the foul mouth's

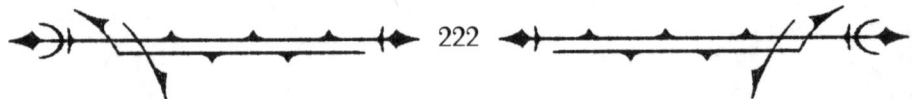

language grew extra foul. By Zenith's stopwatch, the steady stream of insults lasted for over eight minutes. In order to save air and not further enrage Salty Mouth, Zenith tried not to laugh. He failed.

"What's so funny, you asterisk?"

"Nothing. I'm sorry," said Zenith, not sounding sorry at all.

"The hashtag you are." Salty smiled wickedly. "But you will be." She made a loud clicking noise.

From the middle of the humble set of porcelain dinnerware, an upside-down soup bowl scuttled across the pile of treasure on four butter knife legs and began poking Zenith's impenetrable boots with two salad fork arms. Zenith tried kicking the crockery crab away, but only angered it. It attacked his legs, where the material of his suit was much thinner. Zenith could feel the tines. He ignored the pain and checked the time. Suddenly only two minutes were left before he needed to exit.

"Get him, my pet!" Salty Mouth laughed. "*Now* you're sorry, you Firman weakling!" Zenith fought the crab one-handed, holding on to Kreeble with the other while straining toward the portal. He should've moved faster when he'd had the chance. How long did he have? The deflating double air bladder had shifted inside his helmet and was blocking his view of the stopwatch.

Just as he reached the portal, the crab punctured his suit and his skin. Zenith cried out in pain. Salty Mouth roared with laughter. The boy dove through the guffawing gateway to the bottom of the Scalding Sea.

He patted Kreeble's stone belly. She shed her stone skin and swam upward. Zenith was certain he had less than the seven minutes of air he needed to reach the surface. And that ideal time was based on the usual buoyancy of his diving suit, which was now filling with water, slowing his ascent. He swam as hard as he could to compensate, though he was using even more air to do so. Zenith heard precious seconds tick away, heard the hiss of air diminish. He gazed toward the faraway lime green surface as his lungs began to ache. A gray veil clouded his vision. Then all was black.

Seasick

THE AFTERLIFE IS *smelly*, thought Zenith. He opened his eyes. *And rustic*. He lay on a wooden cot in a wooden hut. He heard ocean waves. A potbellied stove kept the windowless room warm, and a pot of simmering fish heads provided the aroma. Kreeble sat perched on the foot of the bed. She said, "He is awake."

Flaajeb entered, looking much older but just as sour as he had twenty-six years ago. "You owe me a new diving suit. And three weeks' rent." He clapped Zenith's ankle through the woolen blanket. "Time to get up and get out. You can pay Jafabel on your way home."

Zenith rubbed his aching head. "Three weeks?"

Flaajeb tossed Zenith his clothes. "That's how long you've been sick with the twists. Not even charging you for all the time wasted waiting for your late arrival. Because I've got a tender heart." Flaajeb attempted a smile.

Zenith dressed hastily. Three extra weeks in GrahBhag was less than a day back home. But each minute on Grawlix was a month on Earth. How many extra seconds had he spent there? What did that add up to in Earth time? There was no time for speculation or calculation. Three weeks on GrahBhag plus unknown extra seconds on Grawlix equaled *get-home-now.*

Zenith blurted, "Thanks," and bolted from Flaajeb's seaside shack. Then, turning back, he said, "Kreeble, I'm sorry. I have to go home. Right now."

Kreeble smiled and nodded. "We each have a home to which we must return."

Zenith hurtled up the nearest stairs and climbed through the streets of Bobbin, then sprinted across Whichway Woods and up the hill, pausing only to feed blood to Dry Mouth's portal before jumping inside. Hiding his face, he ignored the mouths' interrogations and climbed toward the open clasp.

He stopped beneath the opening. *Please don't let*

me be too late. Then he hoisted himself up and out of the horrible bag.

Zenith tumbled onto a wooden surface with a loud *clunk*. He quickly realized this was his own front porch. Footsteps approached from inside. He placed the bag upright and untied the string from its clasp, then dashed across the lawn and hid behind the hedge.

His younger self opened the front door and said, "Hello?" before noticing the horrible bag and taking it inside.

Zenith wondered who or what had taken the bag from its hiding place in the park and delivered it to his home. How long had it been there? And would it still be there, undiscovered by younger Zenith, if he himself hadn't caused such a ruckus upon exiting?

He contemplated time travel conundrums till he heard distant voices and the sounds of a struggle. He crept over to the side of the house. Stopping shy of his bedroom window, he heard his younger self say, "My sister's been taken, and it's up to me to get her back."

It's up to both of us, thought Zenith, and he peeked

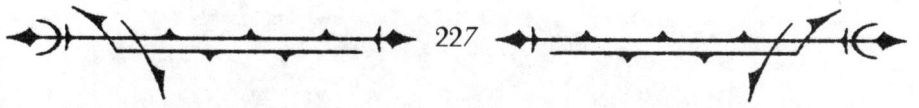

inside. He watched his younger self disappear inside the horrible bag. Zenith entered the empty house, going directly to his bedroom. He took a deep breath, camouflaged his face with his scarf, then followed himself into the world of GrahBhag.

Shadow

ZENITH'S HEART SWELLED as he sat hidden, watching Kreeble, Krobble, Kribble, and Krone share a mushroom supper in the center of the clearing they called home. Their meal was interrupted by two voices approaching from the south. The gargoyles scrambled atop the four columns and transformed into stone.

Younger Zenith and teenage Apogee entered, quarreled, and were caught on the spinning stone in the center of the clearing. As the siblings wandered off to become lost, Zenith followed, saying a silent goodbye to his frozen gargoyle friends.

He shadowed his sister and self for several hours, and after Apogee was recaptured by the Shlurp, he trailed behind younger Zenith as he made his alliance with Kreeble and met Raggedy Albert. Zenith remained unseen and mostly undetected. Only once

did he stray too close, prompting Albert to pause as he led the others to his cabin.

Zenith kept a greater distance through young Zenith's escape from Raggedy Albert, his chalk-stealing caper at the Collectory, and his trek to Stoating. But despite the agony in his wrist and the dirge-like chant of *Aah Bah Cee* in his head, Zenith crept closer and hid behind one of the lava pillars as the Merging ceremony reached the point when the Wurm seemed to swallow teenage Apogee. He felt a surge of pride as younger Zenith reached for the chalkboard. And then, for a moment, the whole world glowed white.

As spots swam before Zenith's eyes, the chant in his head changed from lament to celebration. *Aahbahcee aahbahcee AaahBaahCeeeeee!*

What trick is this? hissed the spirit of Draulic. *This shapeshifting witch is the One? I don't believe it!*

Aah Bah Cee! insisted the spirit of the blanket.

You say you snuggled with this whelp? Nonsense! You're a fool or a liar. Now let me feed!

The Wurm's cloak convulsed. *AAH BAH CEE! What are you doing? Stop! I demand you stop! AAHBAHCEE AAHBAHCEE AAHBAHCEE!*

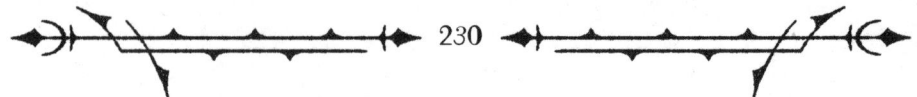

The cloak's color darkened from bright red to mottled purple as its internal battle raged. The blanket's chant became a scream of anger and defiance. The voice of Draulic shrieked in frustration and rage. A piercing, multivoiced screech exploded from the Wurm as it struggled, thrashed, and finally crumpled, releasing little Apogee unharmed.

As the outraged guests pursued Kreeble and the escaping siblings, Zenith hid under the nearest table, concealing himself beneath the overhanging animal pelt tablecloth. He scarcely breathed, lest the Wurm—or was it now already the Wraith?—discover him. When he peeked out again, he alone remained.

By now, young Zenith and even younger Apogee would be safely back on Earth, and he hurried to join them. But he'd forgotten that his younger self had destroyed the bridge over Gaping Gorge to evade the pack of pursuing Shlurps, and Zenith now had to use a longer, less direct route to return home.

By the time he got there, the chamber of the foul mouths was dark. Too dark. The opening of the bag was unexpectedly closed. All three mouths insisted they hadn't pulled any tricks. Then Zenith realized they weren't to blame. He was. When his younger

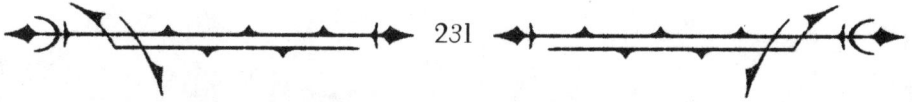

self had returned, one of the first things he'd done was to wrap his bicycle chain around the bag. Over the weeks to come, young Zenith would use various locks to keep Apogee from breaking back into the horrible bag.

And now those locks were going to stop Zenith from breaking out.

Firman in a Foreign Land

ZENITH HAD FOLLOWED his younger self on this first misadventure to make sure nothing had changed, but now that things had happened exactly as he'd remembered, he felt incredibly stupid. His next chance to escape from GrahBhag would come when the bag was open at the start of the siblings' second journey. But that was a scant chance, as the bag would quickly be locked up in police custody once his parents discovered their children's absence. And just how quickly had that discovery occurred? His parents had planned to be out for hours, but they suspected something was wrong before they left. What if worry had driven them to return early? Worse yet, what if Zenith took a chance and timed his passage such that he tumbled through the portal and collided with Apogee or his younger self? How might that alter their collective future?

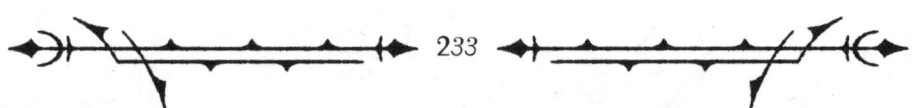

He considered speeding time up by going back to Grawlix. But minutes there were years on GrahBhag, leaving little room for error. His last trip had been full of errors. Plus, once Muncie began experimenting and the portal became destabilized, there was no telling where it might lead. He might end up in toxic Gausia.

Resigned to staying in GrahBhag, Zenith returned to Bobbin. He'd left in such haste that he'd neglected to pay his debt to Flaajeb. He descended through the cliffside city to Flaajeb's seaside shack. Instead of a hearty handshake, the gruff fisherman greeted him by twisting Zenith's wrist around his back and asking where his money was.

Zenith yelped, "In my pocket!"

Releasing him, Flaajeb ushered Zenith inside and growled, "It's supposed to be with Jafabel."

Rubbing his wrist, Zenith said, "I thought you'd like to be paid directly."

Flaajeb stirred his fish head soup. "What need have I of money? With my own hands I catch the food I eat; I built the house I sleep in."

Zenith stared at his feet and then at Flaajeb's crudely constructed table, upon which sat a deck of

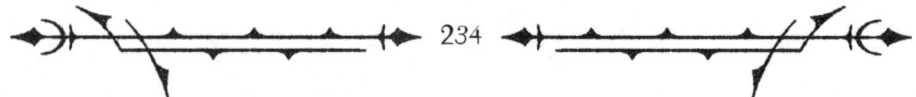

playing cards. "Hey, is that Abund—I mean, is that Dan Bun?"

The grim old fisherman's face lit up. Suddenly, he was a schoolboy. "You know the game?"

Several hours and many Dan Bun games later, a deal was struck over bowls of Flaajeb's soup, which tasted worlds better than it smelled. Zenith agreed to visit the fisherman regularly for Dan Bun tournaments, and in exchange, Flaajeb would teach him that wrist-hold and other maneuvers that might prove useful when the future Final Battle for the Collectory eventually took place.

Climbing back up to Bobbin proper, Zenith visited Jafabel. The shopkeeper was stooped and slow, but her mind was as sharp as it had been twenty-six GrahBhagian years earlier. She was pleased to settle the debt, but it did little to alleviate the sorry state of her affairs. During the era of the Wurm, the past had gone out of favor. Zenith refrained from asking for his old job back. Instead, he overpaid for a Firman ballpoint pen and a spiral notebook with a star-and-rainbow pattern that reminded him of Apogee.

On his way out, he ran into Kreeble coming in. Delighted, Zenith went to hug her, then halted.

Kreeble was not one for displays of affection. He said, "What are you doing here?"

"Lingering in the doorway, waiting for you to get out of my way."

"I mean, why are you here instead of with the other gargoyles?"

Kreeble sighed. "After seeing you recovered from the twists, I returned to my family only to find myself already there. The sight of two Kreebles was enough to shock them all into stone, including my other self."

"Yeah, I was afraid the same thing would happen with my family. The shock, not the turning to stone."

"Thank you for clarifying," said Kreeble. "I wish you had also clarified how far we were time traveling in GrahBhagian years rather than Firman months. You talked so often of saving your sister from the Wurmhole that I assumed that was the time to which we were returning."

Zenith grimaced. "Sorry. I should've made things clearer. And I should've thought of the double Kreeble problem." He explained how his plan had been to shadow his younger self and how it had backfired.

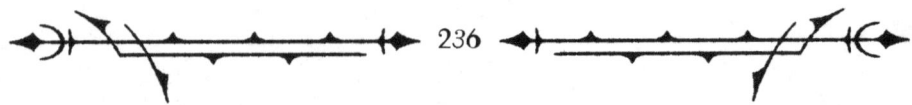

"So, your ill-conceived scheme has stranded us both."

Zenith nodded in apology, then said, "You're working for Jafabel now?"

"I am employed by her but hardly working. With business so slow, I am more of a burden than a help."

"If I wasn't about to become 'Wanted: Dead, Alive, or Eaten,' we could revive the old street performance."

Kreeble stroked her chin. "I might be able to find some other way to exploit your Firman status." She gestured for him to follow her into the shop. "And failing that, I can always turn you in for the reward."

Zenith laughed. "Kreeble! You told a joke." His smile faded. "That was a joke, right?"

Wadding

AFTER A FAREWELL meal and promises to visit, Zenith and Kreeble left Jafabel and Bobbin behind. Zenith suggested they try their luck in Wadding, the village closest to the Collectory. As before, he relied upon his voluminous scarf to conceal his identity. But now that the Poison One and the Dread Outlaw Maelstrom had defeated the Wurm, simply being Firman was enough to antagonize some GrahBhagians.

Kreeble was able to turn this animosity to their advantage. She secured a job for Zenith at the Thirsty Cleric, a public house run by a two-foot-tall blue jay named Bowt. Zenith's duties included sweeping the floor, emptying the spittoons, and sanitizing the oddly equipped restrooms. But his primary function was provoking the tavern's rowdier patrons with his mere Firman presence. Bowt considered the ensuing tussles to be a boon. The cost of any breakage was offset by the increase in business, as his clients enjoyed the spectacle of a good brawl and wagered on the outcomes. And Bowt relished rooting for whoever appeared to be the underdog, usually Zenith.

Initially, Zenith thought these skirmishes would be good practice for the larger battle to come. Many scrapes and bruises later, he wasn't so sure. But under Flaajeb's ongoing tutelage, he eventually learned to give as good as he got.

He shared a small apartment over the pub with Kreeble, who behaved both as roommate and pet, complaining when Zenith didn't do his share of the cleaning, then creating a huge mess by burrowing into the underside of their sofa. Zenith enjoyed Kreeble's cooking, and Kreeble relished Zenith's ear grits. Savoring them one evening, she said, "They are developing an oaky, robust flavor as you age."

Eager to avoid the kind of memory loss Kevin had experienced, Zenith wrote each night in his notebook about his life back on Earth, finishing each entry with a sketch of the horrible bag. He frequently flipped back to earlier entries, reliving cherished moments with his family until he grew too downhearted to continue. On days off, he often visited Flaajeb and Jafabel, especially during winter when Kreeble spent most of her time in stone hibernation.

Two years passed before the notorious Maelstrom siblings returned. Word of their second adventure circulated in secondhand retellings that strayed wildly from actual events. Zenith overheard one wide-eyed pub patron tell a fascinated crowd, "Then the Poison One levitated and flew through the air."

"I were there too!" said a blue-haired beast. "And before the Poison One flew off, I saw the Dread Outlaw Maelstrom tear two kiddies apart with his bare hands . . . and eat 'em!" Zenith had to bite down on his scarf to stop from laughing.

Tumultuous times followed as GrahBhag was beset by raids from Apogee's rebels, disturbances from bizarre quantum creatures, and the destructive quakes caused by the Scribe's experiments with String Theory. When one such quake demolished a section of Wadding, Zenith and the pub's brawnier patrons put their differences aside, working together to clear the wreckage and rescue trapped villagers.

Public opinion shifted in favor of the rebels once they began to share their plunder with the populace.

Curses directed toward the Poison One were supplanted by warm words about the Warrior Witch. A network of collaborators arose in every village, and Zenith and Kreeble joined the Wadding branch.

Soon enough, four years had passed. Zenith had grown straight and tall, and though he would never best Musclehead in a bodybuilding competition, his physique had been toned by years of brawling. Those on the side of the nascent rebellion now held Firmankind in high regard, and patrons who had started as Zenith's sparring partners had become friends. He felt wistful about leaving them behind when he returned to what he now thought of as his first, but not only, home. But as the fateful day of Apogee's revolt approached, melancholy was replaced by excitement over the chance to finally set things right. He had begun this journey to save Apogee, but now the stakes seemed even higher.

Battle and Catastrophe

THIS TIME, ZENITH was right in the middle of the Final Battle for the Collectory, the fight he'd previously only overheard from inside Muncie's tent. Apogee's rebels recruited the villagers of Wadding to fight beside them. The Royal Guard was surprised by the early morning attack, with half the brigade still in their skivvies. Little blood was shed before they surrendered.

As he exchanged hearty backslaps with his rowdy friends, Zenith turned to Kreeble and said, "The 'thick of battle' was rather thin, wasn't it?"

The gargoyle drew his attention to the far side of the celebrating crowd. "While you amuse yourself with your Firman expressions, your sister and her entourage are leaving us behind."

Zenith saw Apogee, Old Timer, the rebels, and

various villagers were indeed already halfway to the Collectory. He and Kreeble sought to catch up, with the gargoyle easily weaving through small gaps in the crowd, and Zenith falling farther and farther behind. Finally breaking free, he ran as fast as he could up the incline toward the circle of rocks. He heard the rebels' celebratory cheers die away as the newly created Wurmhole raced toward his sister.

Zenith cursed and pumped his legs harder. Why had he joined the battle when he should've just camped out on the ridgeline? After four years of waiting, he was going to be five seconds too late. He heard younger Zenith say, "Oh, Geegee. We both know that's not true," and the rebels gasping as his younger self and younger Kreeble were swallowed by the Wurmhole, leaving Apogee vulnerable. He crested the hill, afraid of what he might see.

Apogee stood where she had when Zenith had been spirited away. The Wurmhole strained toward her, but Krobble, Musclehead, and Stickyfingers all gripped the hem of its toxic cloak. The gargoyle's claws were transformed into stone, and the rebels' hands were encased in Stickyfingers's protective blue goo. Zenith had a moment of ecstatic happiness watching the others protect Apogee. And then everything fell apart.

An intense vibration rippled from the base of the Collectory's trunk along each set of stitches as, all at once, the seams ripped open and a cacophonous musical chord resounded throughout the valley.

The rocks along the ridgeline toppled, as did most of the rebels, including Zenith. Tumbling downhill, he stopped mere inches from a still-widening crevasse. From this newly created portal scuttled a crockery crab like the one that had punctured his dive suit in Grawlix, followed by hundreds of its brethren. Zenith scrambled out of the way, then stood and marveled at the unfolding chaos. Muncie's warped version of String Theory had unstrung GrahBhag.

A witchy woman in black robes rode out of one gateway on a saddled beast with the body of a horse and the head of a lion. A six-foot-tall rabbit with striped fur of red, white, black, and brown, the spitting image of Dan Bun, skipped forth from another gap. The largest breach was still widening when the tip of an immense, pointy head protruded, followed by a single glaring eye.

The senselessness of it all made Zenith grateful for the one recognizable point of reference—the reappearance of the two foul mouths, Little and Dry, still vomiting up the same toxic glop from their manifestation in Whichway Woods. Then he imagined the lethal gunk incinerating his sister and whipped around to locate her amid the madness.

Apogee was astride Musclehead's broad shoulders, directing the unseeing bodybuilder as he pummeled a flock of winged serpents. Musclehead's goo-encrusted fists were protected, but several snakes nonetheless embedded their fangs in the vulnerable flesh of his torso. None had bitten Apogee, yet.

Zenith ran toward her, evading fissures and the otherworldly fiends spilling forth. Then GrahBhag's very own fiend floated into view. The Wurmhole stopped in front of his sister and her fighter, spinning in place for a moment before tilting the wide bottom of its funnel upward. The blackness inside was deep and wide and ready to welcome Apogee.

Under a Rock

THE WURMHOLE'S UPTURNED cloak contracted, then sucked the attacking serpents into its endless blackness, including three with fangs embedded in Musclehead's rippling chest.

Musclehead dropped his fists and asked Apogee, "Where'd they go?"

Without breaking his stride, Zenith snatched his sister from the bodybuilder's shoulders. Musclehead cried, "Hey! Where'd *you* go?"

Zenith shouted, "I've got her! Follow the sound of my voice!" As Apogee struggled in his arms, he added, "Don't worry, I'm a friend."

Musclehead ran after him. "Come back with our leader!"

"I'm taking her to safety." But was he? How? Where?

There! At the top of the hill, Kreeble was waving

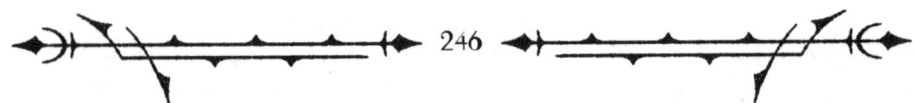

him on as Krobble propped up a boulder from the toppled circle of rocks. Beneath the boulder, Zenith saw an opening. Still carrying Apogee, he descended a short slope into a subterranean chamber. He placed his squirming sister on the ground, but before he could say a word, Musclehead grabbed him. Although the muscleman's face was concealed by his overdeveloped physique, the anger in his voice was unmistakable.

"Explain yourself, 'friend.'" Musclehead's meaty hands felt around Zenith's chest. "Also, explain this large scarf."

Zenith pulled the cloth down off his face and said, "Apogee Maelstrom, what if I told you I had a message from your brother?"

Apogee narrowed her eyes. Her tongue protruded slightly from between her lips. "I'd say you *are* my brother, despite the fact you're too tall and weirdly muscular. The scar on your wrist and the one above your ear give you away."

Zenith grinned. "Right as always, Geegee." The Maelstrom siblings embraced.

"Can someone explain what's going on?" said Musclehead.

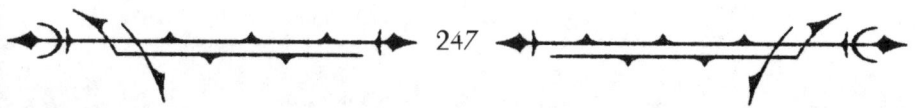

Kreeble said, "I have tried explaining to Krobble, and she is quite confused."

"*I'm* confused," said Zenith. "And I lived through it." He briefly recounted the events of the past four years that everyone but Kreeble had experienced as a matter of seconds. He relayed the encounters with Draulic, the Wurm's creation, and what he'd "heard" of the creature's thoughts. All eyes turned to Apogee when Zenith revealed that it wasn't one monolithic monster, but two entities coexisting within the bloodstained cloak that had once been her snuggle blanket.

Apogee stared at the ground and said, "I didn't know. Maybe I should have guessed. But I didn't." Everyone was still.

Finally, Musclehead said, "So, did you change events or just witness what was going to happen anyway?"

Zenith shrugged. "Both, maybe? If you want to talk about time travel conundrums, ask Schrödinger."

"Schrödinger's *Cat*," said a female voice from deeper in the tunnel. Kevin Churl strode forward carrying the cat in her silver box. The lid had been removed, permanently.

Kevin looked Zenith over. "Couldn't stand the

fact I was taller, huh? Had to resort to time travel."

Schrödinger's Cat said, "This tunnel connects to the rest of the underground network. We can use it to escape."

Musclehead reached for his pint-size leader and said, "What are we waiting for?" Apogee approached Musclehead while the others started down the passageway. Zenith was tempted to follow.

"Hold on," he said. "I might have a way to defeat the Wurm . . . hole."

This caused a commotion, which Apogee halted with a sharp "Quiet." More softly, she said, "Go on, Nit."

Zenith paced, rubbing his A-shaped scar. "Well, as I said, when It gets in my head, I hear two voices. The thing that used to be Draulic is greedy and malicious and initially seemed to be stronger. But the other entity, the one from your neglected blanket, stopped the Draulic part from feeding on you at the Merging. Then the Wurm stopped feeding altogether, and I think that further weakened Draulic. The Wraith simply wandered around, striking out in anger." He turned to Apogee. "I think the blanket part was frustrated It had found you only to lose you again. Getting you back again has become Its obsession."

"Which is why we need to get away from here," said Musclehead. "Before It gets another chance to feed on you."

"I don't think It ever wanted that," said Zenith. "The insatiable Draulic part, sure, but the spirit of the blanket seems to be more in control now. I tamed the wild baseball bat by holding it. That's what it needed. This may seem crazy, but I don't think the Wurm wants to hurt you. I think It needs to hold you."

Musclehead laughed derisively. "You *are* crazy! You've done nothing but try to keep your sister away from the Wraith, and now you want her to leap into Its arms? Wait, does the blasted thing have arms?"

"Not anymore," said Schrödinger's Cat. "All this talk of the 'Wurm' and the 'Wraith' is beside the point. Maelstrom used the Collectory to transform It into the Wurmhole, and we have no idea what this new creature wants."

"I'm not sure that's true," said Zenith. "It sucked up the flying snakes attacking Musclehead and Apogee, protecting her."

"Or saving her for Itself," said Kreeble.

Kevin said, "Even if Wurm Part A wants hugs, who's to say Wurm Part B won't go in for a bite?"

Musclehead turned to Apogee. "Let's get out of here, regroup with the others, and figure out a new battle plan."

"New battles won't matter," said Zenith. "We can't win the war. Apogee can't age herself back up. We can't save GrahBhag. Not with the Wurmhole in the way."

Kevin said, "'We'? I thought you didn't want to fight for GrahBhag."

"GrahBhag has been my home for four years." Zenith thought of the rowdy, rough gang from the Thirsty Cleric, his tough but fair boss, Bowt. Kind Jafabel and her curmudgeonly cousin Flaajeb. Wise Krone, strong Krobble, sensitive Kribble, and of course, his first and most enduring ally, Kreeble. Looking at her, he said, "I have family here."

Kreeble stared back blankly. "You seem to be waiting for a reciprocal emotional response." She gave Zenith a perfunctory pat on the hand.

"Commander Apogee, please," Musclehead said. "You can't be serious about trying what your brother's suggesting."

Apogee stared at the cavern floor, tongue protruding from between her lips. "Zenith's idea is just one piece of the puzzle." She turned to her brother and smiled. "But I see how the other pieces might fall into place."

Apologies

KROBBLE PUSHED BACK the boulder protecting the tunnel's entrance. Zenith and Kreeble peered out, surveying the continuing chaos created by the quake.

Zenith whispered, "Do you see It?"

Kreeble pointed. "There."

The Wurmhole spun across the hillside, navigating around the seam where the foul mouths still spewed Gausia's toxic acid and avoiding the breach from which the tremendous cyclops still peeked.

Zenith and Kreeble exited the tunnel, followed by Krobble, Kevin, Musclehead, and Apogee. The group advanced, with Apogee quickly overtaking the lead.

The Wurmhole spun faster, soaring toward Apogee. Zenith fought the impulse to intercept the fiend. He pictured the Wurmhole transporting

Apogee to another time and place. Or worse, he imagined it crushing her bones as it feasted on the meal Draulic craved.

But Zenith finally understood. As Apogee had once said, she wasn't some "distressed damsel" needing rescue. She'd liberated the inmates of Eternity Tower. They'd chosen her to lead the GrahBhagian rebellion. Whoever Apogee had become during her time in GrahBhag, she had always been the girl with the strength and heart to battle monsters and protect her impetuous brother from his worst instincts. Watching his sister step forward, Zenith was in awe.

Apogee's voice was clear and confident. "There you are!" The Wurmhole levitated, spinning in place. "Now, don't run away." She hustled forward and snatched its hem with both hands, unscathed. It twirled and unfurled into a flat fabric rectangle, its interdimensional powers apparently dispelled. But then it fought the hold she had on it, contorting madly. It twisted and strained with all the ferocity of the Great Wurm, all the anguish of the Wraith. But Apogee held firm till it exhausted its furor. She shook it vigorously, her tongue protruding with the effort.

Apogee then wrapped it around her head and

body, creating a hood by clasping the cloth beneath her chin. The Wurm's remaining resistance melted away. The cloak tightened around Apogee's body as the excess fabric trailing out behind her slithered across the ground and gathered at her feet. The group moved in closer. Apogee shook her head to stop them. They retreated, though Zenith was the most reluctant to do so.

The black symbols on the cloak's surface shifted from mathematical equations to something simpler—letters in the repeated pattern of *A, A, A, B, B, B, C, C, C*. Zenith thought he heard the familiar chant in his head, gentler now. He half expected the cloth's crimson color to revert to the original mauve, but the blood it had spilled couldn't be expunged so easily.

Apogee comforted the creature that had once been her beloved blanket. "I'm sorry," she said quietly. "I shouldn't have abandoned you. It's just, I felt so guilty about what happened to Nit at the pond, and I kind of blamed you too. That was wrong." She began to loosen its grip on her. The Wurm resisted, coiling tighter around her tiny legs. She soothed it. "It's okay, it's okay. I'm here now." She gently detached it. "I'm so sorry. I should've taken you home.

I should've kept you out of trouble." She gathered the entire bulk of the blanket in her little arms the best she could, holding and caressing it. "I should've saved you." One tear escaped and was absorbed by the blanket. "But now it's too late."

Apogee flung it into a geyser of molten acid erupting from the foul mouths. Its cry penetrated Zenith from without and within. It was everything: outrage and betrayal and hurt and sorrow and malice and despair and perhaps, briefly, remorse. And then the shriek was promptly silenced as the Great and Holey Wurm, in all Its Allfullness, was nothing but ash.

New Order

THE DAYS FOLLOWING the Wurm's demise were turbulent and joyous. With their master destroyed and control of the Collectory lost, the Royal Guard quickly surrendered to the rebels. The clerics and other trolls in positions of power fled to parts unknown.

"Rumor has it," said Loose Lips, "they've snuck through one of the gaps in the stitches and escaped to another world."

"I hope it's Gausia," replied Zenith.

Before those stitches could be repaired and the breaches closed, the newly constituted People's Guard, led by Commander Musclehead, had to help the otherworldly visitors who wished to return to their own worlds. Most were eager to go home, but a few preferred to remain in GrahBhag, including the six-foot-tall rabbit everyone now called Dan Bun, who decided to stay and bask in his newfound fame.

The story of the Warrior Witch's final confrontation with the Great and Holey Wurm grew more fantastical as it spread across GrahBhag. Apogee had purportedly worked some ancient magic to lay her bare hands on the burning surface of the beast, which she then either shredded into pieces, banished to some nether realm, or threw into the sun. Few knew the Wurm hadn't been defeated by magic or brute strength, but through a combination of Apogee's tenderness and cunning.

Apogee's enhanced reputation came in handy as she, Old Timer, and the rest of the rebels marched to Binding to form a new government. Her comrades anticipated Apogee's coronation, but she declined, stating that no one should be crowned and that everyone should participate in their own governance. Subsequent weeks of arguments among the fractious factions gave way to hard-won compromises. The result was a new democratic constitution, and more importantly, the rebirth of hope.

Zenith and Kevin spent this time searching the Collectory for the one slate among many that kept Apogee frozen at the age of four. They had occasional help from Schrödinger's Cat and the repentant Scribe, both of whom were systematically editing the scientific "enhancements" to GrahBhag and weeding out the thorny String Theory additions entirely. They spent many hours with whiskers and beak buried in the pages of the physics book, which appeared delighted to be so needed.

Kevin eventually found the long-sought-after chalkboard. Apogee was recalled from Binding, and early one morning the Maelstrom siblings met under the shimmering canopy of the Collectory. They grabbed two pieces of iridescent, enchanted chalk from a new heaping pile on Muncie's desk, restored to its rightful place nearby. Schrödinger's Cat had won the Scribe's admiration by suggesting he use his final stub to write a message imbuing the chalk with the power to self-regenerate, thus ensuring that the enchanted chalk would never again be in short supply.

Zenith hoisted Apogee into the branches of the

Collectory, both of them agreeing it was safer to leave their chalkboard attached and edit it in place. Zenith hoped it wouldn't be the last thing they agreed on, but he feared they had different ideas about the Revisions and Additions that needed to be written.

Revisions and Additions

APOGEE SCRAMBLED UP the branches faster than Zenith. "Geegee! Wait up." For once she listened to him, sitting down on a thick branch and swinging her little legs impatiently. He caught up and sat beside her. "You know, we haven't talked about how we're going to change the chalkboard."

Apogee scowled and crossed her arms. "What's there to talk about?"

"Well . . ." Zenith scratched the scar above his left ear. "Let's start with why you aged yourself up in the first place. When I time traveled, I went back to the day of the accident on Kalikov Pond. I saw the original, unaltered accident."

Apogee's face fell. "You . . ."

"I know you weren't there when the ice broke. You lost your beloved blanket and went after it."

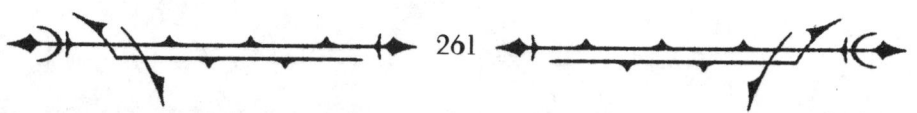

"Zenith, I—"

"And I heard you talk with Mom in the hospital and with younger, unconscious me."

"How did you—"

"I was hiding behind the privacy curtain. Not important. What matters is I know how guilty you felt and what you sacrificed to make things right." Zenith took Apogee's hands in his. "You skipped half your childhood, half of your life so far, to save mine. I'm eternally grateful. I can never repay you. But, Geegee, you can't do it again. You're too smart to be so stupid."

Apogee pulled her hands away. "I don't want to argue, Nit."

"Neither do I. You've earned the right to be whatever age you want. You want to be a fourteen-year-old, fine with me. But do it for yourself, not out of some misguided idea you need to be the older one to keep me out of danger." He gestured to his now teenage self. "If that's your reason, you're going to have to aim even older. Skip over most of your teen years as well as your childhood.

"And it's not necessary. Remember, after I made you younger you *still* saved me from the pond. You

called for help using that noisy little whistle Mom gave you. You're the most capable person I've ever met, regardless of age. I mean, you led a successful rebellion as a pipsqueak."

Apogee's attempt to suppress a smile failed. "True."

"You can look out for me whatever age you choose." He gave her a brief tickle under the armpit. "And I'll look out for you."

Apogee batted his hand away as she suppressed a giggle. "Okay, Nit. You win. I'll go back and live the years I skipped. But only if you do the same."

"What?" Zenith shook his head. "Geegee, no. I didn't skip over anything."

"Yes, you did. You skipped over Mom and Dad teaching you to drive, and school dances, and flunking algebra." Zenith made a face as Apogee continued. "You skipped over everything a typical teen should experience. You did the same thing I did—you sacrificed your life to save mine."

Zenith stroked his chin. "I don't know, Geegee. I'm not sure I want to start puberty all over again . . ."

Apogee elbowed him in the ribs. "This time, you'll have me to point out how awkward you look."

He kissed the top of her head. "Sold."

They climbed together to the branch that contained their chalkboard. Apogee pulled the branch toward them, careful not to pluck it free. Zenith used the hem of his shirt to erase the second sentence, which eliminated his psychic knowledge of Apogee's whereabouts, and the third sentence, thereby freeing Hugh from his servitude. There was one sentence left, written in aqua blue chalk, which read, "Zenith Maelstrom has a four-year-old sister named Apogee."

The siblings stared at each other, stumped. It was a puzzle even Apogee couldn't solve. How could they change their ages without ending up developmentally frozen?

"Let's go get Schrödinger's Cat," said Zenith.

Apogee nodded. "And Muncie."

They found the Scribe and his new apprentice and explained their problem. The bird and the cat exchanged a glance, then spoke as one. "Yetkinbroska."

"What?" said Zenith.

"Huh?" said Apogee.

"This is a GrahBhagian word," said Muncie. "Translated it means 'a prepubescent youngling who

will soon become a fine adult.' The process of aging is intrinsic to the word's definition."

"Perfect," said Zenith.

"Wait," said Apogee. "Are you sure we won't just get stuck as preteens?"

"Don't worry," said Zenith. "We'll spell it out."

"A word of warning," said Schrödinger's Cat. "It's a vague term, and there's no telling which of you will end up the eldest."

The siblings' eyes met.

"Are you thinking what I'm thinking?" Apogee said.

Zenith grinned.

A short time later, Apogee and Zenith hopped down from the Collectory's lowest branches. Loose Lips and Stickyfingers gasped as the two approached.

Nervously, Musclehead said, "Is the Warrior Witch too big to ride on my shoulders?"

"No worries there," said Stickyfingers. "She's only gained a few inches. But the other Maelstrom . . ."

"Is half the man he was," added Loose Lips.

As they passed by the rebels, Zenith said, "More like two-thirds."

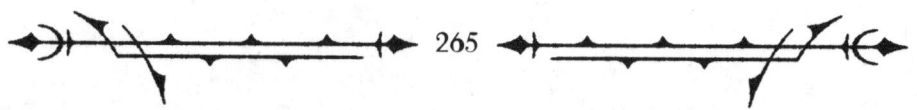

"His voice is so squeaky," said Musclehead. "What happened to him?"

"Yeah, what happened?" said Loose Lips as he trailed behind the siblings. "Give us all the juicy details." But the siblings just laughed.

If Loose Lips had sniffed out that one chalkboard among thousands, he could've seen for himself the words written there—"Zenith Maelstrom has a twin sister named Apogee. These two yetkinbroskas age normally at home on Terra Firmament, where they keep each other out of trouble. Or get into it together."

Celebration

THE DAYS FOLLOWING the Maelstrom twins' transformation were filled with festivities. Chancellor Old Timer and the National Assembly insisted on a farewell address from Apogee. In her remarks, she urged GrahBhag to commit to a new future of cooperation, as she and her brother had. A lavish banquet hosted by Treasury Secretary Stickyfingers followed, with the GrahBhagians on their best behavior, which by Firman standards was still somewhat depraved. Press Secretary Loose Lips observed several incidents that would make for juicy gossip, off the record, of course.

Not to be outdone, the Scribe and the Seeker held an elite, candlelit affair under the boughs of the Collectory. Hugh gave each of the twins an emerald green scarf identical to his own. "As thanks for my independence. Though if the need should ever arise, I'm still at your service."

Schrödinger's Cat approached, nudging her now lidless metal box forward with her nose. Inside was a piece of the enchanted chalk. Muncie intoned, "And this is presented in appreciation for the gift of science you have bestowed upon GrahBhag." Considering the geological events that had culminated in what was now known as the Great Quake, Zenith thought science had proved to be more of a curse than a gift, but he kept his opinion to himself.

The next day, Kevin led the twins through Whichway Woods to the gargoyles' clearing. Zenith descended into the catacombs with trepidation, memories of Draulic arising unbidden, but when he saw Kreeble, Krobble, Kribble, and Krone gathered around the fire, his heart swelled and his qualms vanished.

The presence of Apogee Maelstrom had the opposite effect on Kribble. The starstruck gargoyle was so overcome with nervous excitement that he barely nibbled the many fine dishes Krone had prepared. His greedy kin were thrilled to gobble up his share.

Kreeble relayed her version of the Wurm's

destruction, embellishing the role she'd played without diminishing the bravery of the Maelstroms. Kribble whispered to Kevin, who asked Apogee to talk about the rebels' famous Midnight Raid on Gusset Keep. Stories flowed as easily as the elderberry brew till the hour grew late.

Kevin bedded down with the gargoyles, but the siblings, already settling into their twindom, decided to sleep under the still strange but now less sinister sky. The silence that enfolded them was comfortable, and before long they'd surrendered to drowsiness. Later, Apogee shook Zenith awake and said, "You were restless. Groaning."

Zenith mumbled, "Dreaming . . . of the bag." He sat up, eyes wide. "The horrible, horrible bag! Where on Earth did you first find it?"

"It found me," Apogee said. "I was tossing and turning, unable to sleep. Hoping impossibly for some way to change what I'd done. Wishing I had stayed and protected you instead of chasing after my blanket. I heard a strange sound on the front porch, opened the door, and there it was."

Zenith said, "Just like me on that day in June. The bag just showed up. And even after I time traveled

and stowed it in Kalikov Park, it still made its way back to our porch for my younger self to discover."

"So, when you left the bag unguarded, someone or some force moved it. Or it moved itself." Apogee shivered. "Somehow it came to us when we were most vulnerable to it. How could that be?"

"I guess we'll never really know how or why it appeared. At least it's safely locked up in police custody now."

Apogee pulled her blanket up tight under her chin. "Yes, but for how long?"

They were both silent. This time their silence was less comforting.

Final Farewell

THE RED SUN had barely risen above the Scalding Sea when the group climbed the hill on the edge of Whichway Woods. Zenith was relieved to see the three gaps in the stitches, exactly where they should have been now that GrahBhag was back to normal, relatively speaking.

"Well," said Apogee, holding her hand out to Kribble. "It was nice meeting you."

The gargoyle emitted a short gurgle and hid behind Krobble.

"And by that he means, 'The pleasure is mutual,'" said Krone.

Zenith said, "For you," and handed a large mason jar to Kreeble. It was filled with a soft waxy substance ranging in color from cream to caramel. "It's my teenage ear grits, harvested over the winters

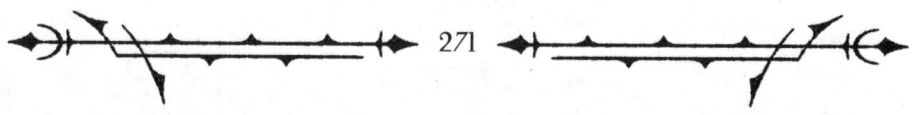

while you hibernated. Hopefully it has that oaky flavor you crave."

Kreeble's eyes filled with tears. "I seem to be having a reciprocal emotional response." She took Zenith's hand in hers. "This is the most thoughtful gift anyone has ever given me." Then noticing Krobble's hungry gaze, she grew less sentimental. "Though I would have preferred it were given in private."

"Oh, jeez," said Kevin. "I didn't know we were doing gifts." He stuck his finger in his ear. "Give me a sec."

Krobble pulled his hand away and embraced him. Kreeble, Kribble, and Krone joined her. Kevin hunched over to hug them, though he didn't need to bend nearly as far as before. A second chalkboard had been added to the Collectory that turned Kevin into a yetkinbroska the same age as the Maelstrom twins and removed the numerous scars inflicted by the Wraith.

Kreeble gestured for Zenith and Apogee to join the group hug. After some time, the three Firmen pulled away, gave a final wave, and without further ado, eased themselves into the hilltop holes that would send them home.

Their farewell with the foul mouths was less tender, though Little Mouth was unusually buoyant as she exclaimed, "Kevin! My conquering hero!"

Zenith said, "There are *three* heroes, actually."

Little Mouth sneered, "Nobody's talking to you."

Dry Mouth cleared her gravelly throat and said, "Thank you, Zenith, Apogee, and Kevin. Your bravery has saved us from torments too terrible to tell. Isn't that right, big sister?"

Big Mouth mumbled, "Um, yes. Thank you."

Dry Mouth whispered, "She's been moody since returning. Won't talk about where she's been."

Little Mouth barked, "All right, Maelstroms, be on your way." Then she purred, "Kevin, you're welcome to stay."

But Kevin led his friends as the three ascended the rope tied to the clasp above. They climbed out and tumbled into the police evidence locker where the horrible bag was stowed. Having learned how to pick a lock during his time with the gargoyles, Kevin made quick work of the padlocked door. The three turned and gazed one final time at the bag, with its mismatched hides, tarnished clasp, and an entire world hidden inside. Then, without a word, Kevin locked the door, and they left the bag behind, exiting the police station unobserved.

They made their way across town, unseen by anyone they knew, and waited inside the bus station for their parents to pick them up. They had used the slate that altered Kevin's age to also explain their absence, writing that the rest of Firmankind believed Kevin and the Maelstrom twins had spent several weeks at summer camp.

While they waited, the three concocted elaborate stories about "Camp Gray Bay." They reimagined GrahBhag's denizens as woodland critters, like the large raven that swiped everyone's pencils and the odd-looking squirrel that liked to be hand-fed while perched on Zenith's shoulder. The rebels became the gossipy kid, the muscle-bound kid, and the kid with fingers sticky from candy. Everyone was strange but harmless, except for the bigger kid who'd developed an unrequited crush on Apogee and had scarred Zenith's wrist when he'd told the boy to back off. Kevin and Apogee had stepped in to save Zenith from further harm, just as they'd both saved him from the pond when the thin ice gave way. In Apogee's words, the three of them had always been "thick thieves."

Zenith knew these invented details weren't necessary. Since they'd inscribed their cover story in the Collectory, their parents would never question its veracity. But unless the three of them took active steps to remember GrahBhag, Camp Gray Bay would soon become their truth as well. Zenith felt certain Apogee would write about their actual experiences each day, accompanied by a small drawing of the bag, and therefore never forget. He was pretty sure Kevin lacked such discipline.

Would Zenith continue the journal he'd started in GrahBhag? He liked to think so. But since the impetuous days when an ice hockey grudge match could have destroyed him and his sister, he'd acquired enough self-knowledge to be skeptical of vows made by the yetkinbroska version of himself. So he'd devised a backup plan in case he lapsed into forgetfulness and new GrahBhagian bizarreness materialized.

As Apogee and Kevin spun yarns about Camp Gray Bay's Albert, the mumbly kid with a fondness for taxidermy, Zenith pulled a small vial from his pocket. It had been created for him by Wadding's resident glassblower, Belafaj, another of Jafabel's cousins. The words "Break in Case of Insanity" were engraved on the vial's surface. Inside was the enchanted chalk, wrapped in a little piece of parchment, like a cloak. Zenith held the vial up to the light and heard what sounded like a faint, low gasp. He told himself it was just the sound of rough parchment against glass, but the picture drawn on that parchment rose unbidden in his mind.

It was an image of the horrible bag.

ACKNOWLEDGMENTS

For their help with this cursed tale, my never-ending thanks to:

Rubin Pfeffer, my literary agent, whose faith, guidance, and support gave me the confidence to expand the world of GrahBhag far beyond its humble beginnings.

John Goldsmith, my animation agent, whose intellect and skill have helped me create a rewarding career making cartoons. And with whom I hope to expand the world of GrahBhag beyond the written page.

Alex Wolfe, my preternaturally perceptive editor, whose comments and suggestions inspired me to tighten the plotting, heighten the horror, and deepen Zenith's emotional journey through his three adventures in GrahBhag.

Rob Valois, Sierra Pregosin, and the rest of the Penguin Workshop team, including Mary Claire Cruz, Shara Hardeson, Caroline Press, Ana Deboo,

Laurel Robinson, and Jessica Nevins. I'm fortunate to have the backing and expertise of such a wonderful group of people.

M. S. Corley, my cover illustrator, who has outdone himself with his tremendous, mesmerizing depiction of the Wretched Wraith. I'm thrilled each time I see the cover.

Jay Myers, who brilliantly gives voice to the Maelstrom siblings and the creatures of GrahBhag, and the entire production team at Penguin Random House Audio and Listening Library, including producer Amber Beard and director Olivia Mackenzie-Smith. I'm eager to hear the audiobook version of this adventure.

Tracy Royce, my wife, first reader, and closest collaborator in all things, whose insight and quick wit improved this story in ways both large and small. I am a better writer, and a better person, because of her.

© Tracy Royce

ROB RENZETTI

is an Emmy Award–winning animation veteran who has worked as a storyboard artist, writer, director, and producer. He created *My Life as a Teenage Robot* for Nickelodeon and most recently served as co-executive producer for Netflix's *Kid Cosmic* and as executive producer on the first two seasons of Disney's *Big City Greens*. He coauthored the #1 *New York Times* best seller *Gravity Falls: Journal 3* and wrote *Onward: Quests of Yore*. Rob spends his spare time playing board games with his wife and corralling their mischievous rabbit, Digby Flopwell.

X/TWITTER: @RobRenzetti
BLUESKY: @robrenzetti.bsky.social
INSTAGRAM: @rob_renzetti
WEBSITE: robrenzetti.com